WHITE ROSE

WHITE ROSE

KIP WILSON

VERSIFY

HOUGHTON MIFFLIN HARCOURT

BOSTON   NEW YORK

Versify® is an imprint of Houghton Mifflin Harcourt Publishing
Company. Versify is a registered trademark of Houghton Mifflin
Harcourt Publishing Company.

hmhbooks.com

The text was set in Sabon LT Std.
Cover design by Sharismar Rodriguez.
Interior design by Sharismar Rodriguez.

The Library of Congress has cataloged the hardcover edition as follows:
Names: Wilson, Kip, author.
Title: White Rose / by Kip Wilson.
Description: Boston : Houghton Mifflin Harcourt, [2019] | Summary:
Tells the story of Sophie Scholl, a young German college student who
challenges the Nazi regime during World War II as part of the White
Rose, a non-violent resistance group. | Includes bibliographical references.
Identifiers: LCCN 2018026607 | Subjects: LCSH: Scholl, Sophie,
1921–1943—Juvenile fiction. | CYAC: Novels in verse. | Scholl, Sophie,
1921–1943—Fiction. | White Rose (German resistance group)—Fiction. |
World War, 1939–1945—Fiction.
Classification: LCC PZ7.5.W56 Wh 2019 | DDC [Fic]—dc23
LC record available at https://lccn.loc.gov/2018026607

ISBN: 978-1-328-59443-3 hardcover
ISBN: 978-0-358-37669-9 paperback

Manufactured in the United States of America
DOC 10 9 8 7 6 5 4 3 2 1
4500814541

PRAISE FOR *WHITE ROSE*

"Candid and absorbing present-tense free verse. . . . [A] strong addition to the canon of WWII fiction." —PUBLISHERS WEEKLY

"Wilson does an exceptional job revealing Sophie's inner thoughts and feelings. . . . Simultaneously uplifting and heartbreaking." —HORN BOOK

"The verses pack an emotional punch. . . . This will be a highly accessible pathway into conversations about the role of women in war and resistance and . . . an insightful addition to any curriculum about resistance in World War II." —THE BULLETIN

"In a searing indictment of silent complicity, *White Rose* shines a light on one remarkable young woman's insistence on the power of truth, no matter the cost. A timely call to resistance." —JOY MCCULLOUGH, author of *Blood Water Paint*

"*White Rose* is a resonant testament to courage. In a time of horrific brutality, young people found a nonviolent way to resist. Told in the form of poetry, the story of their hopes is honored and brought back to life, still relevant today, when regimes that spread hatred are once again thriving, and words are our most powerful defensive weapon." —MARGARITA ENGLE, Newbery Honor winning author of *The Surrender Tree* and the 2017–2019 Young People's Poet Laureate.

"*White Rose* is a deftly plotted, absorbing read. A bold tribute to a brave hero of the German resistance during World War II. Wilson's debut is a triumph!" ——MELANIE CROWDER, author of National Jewish Book Award finalist *Audacity*

"A graceful, moving portrait of a heroic young woman's defiant refusal to remain complicit with Nazi oppression." —JULIE BERRY, Printz Honor–winning author of *The Passion of Dolssa*

"This deeply thought-provoking debut is an important addition to the canon of Holocaust literature for young people; it is sure to inspire discussion and leave a long-standing impact on its readers." —PADMA VENKATRAMAN, award-winning author of *A Time to Dance*

For Megan, Lyra, and Violeta:
May your sisterly love
forever be fierce

For Sophie and Hans:
Allen Gewalten
Zum Trutz sich erhalten
—Johann Wolfgang von Goethe

THE END

FEBRUARY 18, 1943
Gestapo Headquarters

The cars screech to a
halt, officers pull
us out by the arms, haul
us inside and off to
      separate
rooms, my heartbeat
pounding
all the while,
boom-boom,
boom-boom.

They swing
the door shut, unlock
my handcuffs, order
me to sit, rush about with
coats, hats, cases, papers
as I try not
to give in to the
overwhelming,
      sickening
knowledge spreading through me:
the two of us are trapped
in this net because
of me.
Boom-boom,
boom-boom.

I take
a deep breath and prepare
to fight
for our lives.

INTERROGATION

I carefully blend
a cupful of lies
into the bucket of truth
spread out in front of me
as Herr Mohr shoots
question after question,
trying to catch me off-guard.

> *Fräulein Scholl, why were you*
> *carrying*
> *an empty suitcase with*
> *you to the university?*

So I could pick up clean laundry
from home.

> *And why were you at the*
> *university*
> *if you were planning to*
> *head to Ulm?*

So I could let my friend Gisela know
I couldn't meet her for lunch after all.

> *Why were you and your*
> *brother*
> *in the corridor*
> *upstairs?*

So I could show him the Psychological Institute
where I take classes.

His eyes narrow,
his voice icy,
Herr Mohr is good at this,
but he doesn't know
that I'm good, too.
Boom-boom,
boom-boom.

My voice sounds
so calm telling these lies,
I barely recognize
the words as my own.

BEFORE

1935
Fresh Air

I step outside, inhale
the frische Luft deep
into my lungs, make
my way to the Iller,
fourteenth-birthday
sketchbook and
pencils in hand,
alone
but never
lonely.

Slim, tall birch trees reach
up toward the sky
like fingers,
the river rushes
past its banks,
and I sit
on my favorite rock, write
Sophie inside the
new cover, open to
a blank page, draw
the beauty of this world,
one line
at a time.

I KNOW

I might not be
the best-behaved
      girl
I don't want to be
the prettiest
      girl
but

I'm most decidedly
the smartest
      girl.

THE FIVE OF US

In a family with five
teenagers, five
strong opinions, five
lives entwined,
we often travel
as a pack.

Inge!
Hans!
Liesl!
Sophie!
Werner!
Mutti calls the lot
of us to the table, to grace, to
the discussion and
   togetherness
that await.

We traipse
in from the world
beyond our doors, our
young blood
thick as mud as we
talk, sing, laugh,
think
very
much
as
one.

CLIPPED

I won't ever come
close to the German ideal:
    long blond braids
    shining blue eyes
    thoughts of Kinder, Küche, Kirche
                (children, kitchen, church).

Instead I decide
to become the most me
I can.

I bend
my head forward, delight
in the snip, clip of
the scissors, the chunks
of hair quietly cascading
over my shoulders to
the ground below,
the scrape
of the razor at the bottom
of my boyish cut.

I aim to become
not only the most
    me
but the best
    me
I can.

GIFTS FOR MOTHER

It's Mother's Day, and
we five carry
out our plans to free
Mutti from the mundane.

We rise
with the sun, sneak
out of our rooms, divide
the tasks.

Inge and Liesl prepare
eggs, toast, marmalade,
Hans produces a
sheet of paper to compose
an original poem,
Werner and I step
outside, head
for the garden, pick
a bunch of daisies.

Like sunlight warming
the breakfast table,
Mutti shines, reveling
in the glory of her
day before leading
the lot of us
to church, basking

in what truly makes
her happiest:
  the five
  of us.

LEADING BY EXAMPLE

One warm summer night
a group of us gather
around a campfire
       my sisters
       our closest friends
       just us girls.

The fire crackles, shooting
sparks into the dark
night, humming with
possibility, and soon I'm stepping
closer to the flames, prepared
to inspire the others.

Everyone leans
close as I pull the booklet from
my pocket—
       a worn, beloved copy of
       The Lay of the Love and Death of Cornet
         Christoph Rilke
       by Rainer Maria Rilke,
       one of my favorite poets—
and share the story of a
young soldier charging
into battle, sacrificing
       himself
in a moment of true glory.

The girls sigh
in unison, enraptured,
as my voice trembles
over the last line,
of an old woman weeping
over the cornet's death.

May we all become
so noble.

THE BOYS' CAMP

Not far away, my brothers gather
with their friends around their own
campfire.

I imagine
Hans sharing
a Swedish or Russian folk song,
all the boys welcoming
him back
to their sides when he finishes,
tackling him with
open arms, claps on the
backside.

Hans isn't much older than
I am, and yet he's already managed
to charm most everyone who crosses
his path:
   teachers
   parents
   girls
   and even
   boys
some of whom seem
to charm
him right back.

DECREE OF THE FÜHRER
June 1935

Concerning the duration of service
and the strength
of the National Labor Service

to Article 3
of the National Labor Service Law
I hereby decree:

that the duration of service
amounts to six months
until further notice

that the strength of the National Labor Service
is prescribed to be
200,000 men.

The Führer and Reich Chancellor
Adolf Hitler

OUR PARENTS

Vati disapproves of
the service decree like
he disapproves of
everything else
this regime
does.

Mutti
presses her lips
together, shakes
her head, does the
only thing she can: prays.

1937
Leaving Home

Hans stands
    frozen,
surrounded by so many boys brushing
past us, so many bags heaved
up the steps, so much
      enthusiasm
      energy
      testosterone
that the rest of my family and I step
back, blend
into the brick wall with
other well-wishers, lift
our hands in goodbye
as Hans boards
the train bound for Göppingen
for Reichsarbeitsdienst—
    national labor service.

I picture my brother's circle of
admiring friends
here in Ulm, hope
his natural charisma will
attract new ones wherever
he goes,
    no matter
    the circumstances.

One last distracted look
over the crowd, and
Hans's smile breaks
through his cloud of hesitation
before he moves

                              forward

leaving life with us
behind.

POETRY AND PROSE
Letter from Hans, October 1937

Dear family,

The duties here are monotonous,
the days long.

At least in the evenings, a respite
from the ominous thrumming

that comes with the buildup
of so many young men.

We sit around the big table
in the barracks and read, read, read.

I've just finished an exciting novel
by Knittel,

but I'll have to wait
to read Stefan George

until I have the
solitude I so badly need

to let his words
sink in.

CHRISTENING

We've lived
on Olgastraße in
Ulm for a few years now,
in a rented flat
in a lovely building
owned by Jakob Guggenheimer,
a Jewish businessman.

Peppered with
homes, churches, shops,
Olgastraße is
an immense serpent circling
the center of the
city, which means it's
important enough to get
a new name
this year.

They tear
down the old signs, raise
the new ones pronouncing
it as
        Adolf-Hitler-Ring
outside our very doorstep,
despite the fact that our building
houses
several Jewish families

including the Guggenheimers,
the Einsteins.

The Führer makes
no secret of how
much he despises
the Jews, but for our
neighbors to see
this clear sign when they step
outside each morning must
be a baton to the back.

We non-Jews are meant to celebrate
the new name, but this feels
more like a
funeral than a
birth.

RIPPLES

The signs begin
to appear like
mushrooms after a rain.

On the Stuttgarterstraße bridge:
Juden in Ulm nicht erwünscht!
(Jews not wanted in Ulm!)

On park benches:
Nur für Arier
(Only for Aryans)

On Jewish storefronts:
Hier kauft kein Deutscher
(Germans don't shop here)

As if Jews
aren't people like us
at all.

DANCE PARTNERS

Some girls I know take
dancing lessons, curl
their hair, paint
their lips as red
as the flag.

Not me.

My short-as-a-boy's hair flops
over my eyes as I feel
this music, razzle
this jazzy beat, shaking
my hips as I move
across the floor toward *him*
and the kindest eyes I've ever seen.

Everyone else admires
those who know
      how to foxtrot
      how to waltz
      how to tango
but Fritz—
      this boy, a
      freshly minted officer—
seems instead entranced
by strange, ridiculous
me.

ROUNDED UP

Thud, thud, thud.
It's them: the Gestapo.

A blur of black boots and
uniforms sweeps inside, searches
our home, their presence pressing
us against the walls with
no escape.
Boom-boom,
boom-boom.

Vati stands strong as a
fortress, distracting
them while Mutti secrets
away incriminating
books by banned authors—
      Heinrich Heine
      Stefan Zweig
      Thomas Mann—
but the officers are still
suspicious, and they herd
Inge and Werner out the door.
Boom-boom,
boom-boom.

My sister, my brother, scrunched
together in the back of the patrol car,
heads turned toward

home as they're carted
away, away, away.

Boom-boom,
boom-boom.

Boom-boom,
boom-boom.

AFTERMATH

We soon learn there's been
an enormous wave
of arrests throughout Germany
of hundreds of teenagers
including Hans, on his military base
     all of them accused
of getting together
in youth groups other than
the Hitlerjugend
     singing banned songs
     reading banned books
things we do
because
ideas
cannot
be
banned.

Everyone knows
the Hitlerjugend
is the only legal
youth organization in
Germany,

just like everyone knows
the National Socialist Party
is the only legal

political party in
Germany,

but we never expected
our own to get
caught in this trap.

When they ask
me at school if
I'm embarrassed about
my brother's arrest,

my face flames,
not with embarrassment
but with indignation.

A WALK IN THE WOODS

It's a good day to disappear
into nature, to become
one with
      the trees
      the hills
      the sky.

I wouldn't mind slipping
away all by myself, but when
Fritz stops by—
      home for the weekend from
      his first command—
Liesl and I can't tumble out after
him quickly enough.

We amble away
from the city, away
from all angst, into
the heart of a fairy-tale
forest that reminds
me how very
      lucky
we are to live
and breathe
on this great Earth
      flourishing
with wonder.

GUILTY
Letter from Hans, December 1937

Dear family,

Danke, Vati,
for coming

to visit me.
I'm so sorry

you have to endure a child in prison,
so sorry

to have brought this
suffering to the family.

But I am who I am and I promise you:
I'll make everything good again.

TRUTH AND LIES

After whirlwind weeks of
     arrests
     accusations
     realizations
lies begin to settle on the ground
while the truth rises, high
and bright and undeniable.

First Inge, then Werner:
     released
     cleared
          not
          guilty.

But Hans still sits
in prison, can't
even come home, though
it's almost Christmas. I send
him a gift, they refuse
to let him have it.

I want to zoom
across the miles, slap
the warden, rescue
my brother from
this trap.

At home, secret
glances between
Mutti and Vati make
me wonder if there's
something
they're not telling me,
but everything pales
in comparison to
the injustice of
my brother locked
away, and I'm left
with the same indignation,
          bubbling
          blistering
          burning
inside.

BADLY NEEDED ESCAPE

The next time I see
Fritz, winter accompanies
him, coating
the hills with
fresh powder, sending
us indoors, down to a
        smoky
        buzzing
        room
humming with accordion
music and
wine and
song, and Fritz and
I are dancing so
close that a
circle forms
around us, staring
at the two of us,
lost
in each other.

1938
Waiting

Hans is finally released
back to his unit
while awaiting
his court date.

I'm positive
they'll find him
not guilty
when the time comes.

Until then, I wait,
pacing, fists
clenched, mind
racing.

PEN PALS
Letter to Fritz, April 1938

Dear Fritz,

The best thing about
faraway friends is
the letters you can
exchange, but still,
visits
are better.

If you're not coming
home to Ulm this
weekend, then write to
me and let
me know, would you?

Sometimes I imagine
flying over the
    woods
     trees
     hills
from me in Ulm to
    you in Augsburg.

Is it the same for you?

If it is, take the
time right now —

you can,
you're a lieutenant —
and
write
me
back.

THE VERDICT

Acquitted
of
all
charges!
My parents don't share
any details, but I don't care
because Hans is free—
as he should be.

Still, I won't forget
how my brother was
treated.

I pay close attention to
Vati when he calls
the Führer a wolf, ready
to devour our
country whole.

A SURPRISE VISIT

Fritz comes to Ulm
when he can, but I'm too
      impatient
      bored
      reckless
and decide
to sneak off with
my friend Lisa
to visit him on
his base in Augsburg.

The look of surprise
on his face that evening
when he sees
the two of us is
worth all the effort—
until the reality of
nightfall hits
and we admit we have
nowhere to sleep.

I know
he won't leave
us out on the street,
and he doesn't, smuggling
us to his room, matching
my boldness with a share of
his own.

But once there, I can't help but think
how my brother was arrested
on a base just like this, and
the injustice of it all rises
up in me once more, driving
a thick wedge in my
mind between
          us Scholls
and
          them.

THE NORTH

A summer trip up
north with
        Inge
        Werner
        my friends Annelies
        and Lisa
means

        adventure
over the
swelling waves
and chilling breeze of the
North Sea

        inspiration
among the artists at the
colony at Worpswede

        escape
from the once overwhelming
civilization of Ulm, now
        eroding
at its very
foundation with
        soft music turned harsh
        beloved books burned
        true art marked degenerate,
all hints that a terrible future

presses close,
and I fling myself
into nature,

the trees
        so immense
and me
        so very small.

SNAPSHOTS

Fritz loves
the snapshot I send him
from our holiday,
writes back,

> You should see me now.
> I've grown a beard and
> some say I look like a saint,
> some a mutineer from the *Bounty*,
> some Rasputin.

Fritz tells me
not to work too hard
on my return to
everyday life in Ulm,
but I already know
the idyll of
my childhood is
fading away, stomped
flat by something that feels
like doom.

ART CLASS

Back home, holidays over,
and the only thing that has any
appeal is art.

I'd like to become
an artist, but anyone
who wants to do that
must become a fully
realized human being—
something that feels
out of reach
now.

I've got to
work on
myself.

SPILLING THE TRUTH
Letter to Fritz, August 1938

Dear Fritz,

I have to be
honest and
tell you
I can't stay in this relationship as it is now.
I'm too
      young
I'm not
      ready.

I was so happy on
holiday away from home,
but now that I'm
back in Ulm, everything's
heavy
dark
depressing.

I'm sure you know
what I mean.

DEUTSCHLAND ÜBER ALLES

Sometimes I stop, think, wonder.

It's been five years since
Herr Hitler's thundering rise
to power, and
in that time so much has
changed in our small city:

> red flags draped
>> over offices, schools, homes
> armed soldiers blocking entrance to
>> Jewish businesses
> thick, hard dread
>> spilling over the streets
>> sharp as glass.

I shudder, ponder, frown.

What will the
next
five
years
bring?

THE END

FEBRUARY 18, 1943
My Brother

Hours later, with my head spinning
from all the questions,
Herr Mohr pauses, lights up, fills
the room with
the most welcome
smoke.

I breathe
in the nicotine, imagining

Hans

next door, answering
questions about
his service in the Wehrmacht
on the western and eastern fronts,
his medical studies,
our childhood together in
       Forchtenberg
       Ludwigsburg
       Ulm,
the friends we made
there and
here in Munich and
the walls edge closer and
I can't breathe again.
Boom-boom,
boom-boom.

I picture
my brother's pale face,
his fingers tingling, knee bouncing,
and send a wave of courage
his way.

I know Hans will need
the courage,
especially
when they ask about
        what I did today,
when they ask about
        what he did today,
when they ask about
        each of our friends,
when they ask
        questions best answered
with lies.

ROBERT MOHR, GESTAPO INTERROGATOR

I step out
of the interrogation room,
confer
with Inspector Mahler,
the agent questioning
Fräulein Scholl's brother.

We discuss
the students
the leaflets
the suitcase.

Between the two of us,
we'll slip in
the right questions,
trip up
their canned responses,
discover
if they're lying.

THE MAILBOX

Herr Mohr asks the same
questions again and again,
his voice growing sharper,
more insistent each time.

> *Fräulein Scholl, what time*
> *does the morning mail*
> *arrive at your flat?*

I squeeze my eyes shut, imagine
Hans next door being asked
the very same question.

At nine thirty
in the morning.

> *And did you find anything in*
> *your mailbox*
> *this morning? Or did*
> *your brother?*

I didn't. I told my brother he didn't
get any mail either.

Sweat beads up
on the back of my neck.

I hope
our statements
line up.

BEFORE

1939
Hot and Cold

Each time Fritz returns
to Ulm, I feel
confused, conflicted.

Our lives are so different.
I'm seventeen,
        he's twenty-one,
I want to study,
        he already has a career.

Sometimes I'm sure
I don't want
this, don't want

him,

yet sometimes I wonder
what the harm would be in
        conversing
        laughing
        spending
time with someone I truly
care about,
despite
our differences.

SPRINGTIME WISH

With Hans away in Munich,
his first semester studying
medicine, Fritz off training
a fresh batch of new soldiers
for what feels like
        some
        sinister
        purpose,
I'm stuck at home with my
older sisters, parents, younger brother.

Germany might not be
at war, but this doesn't
feel like peace, and
the heavy clouds over Ulm make
me want to float
away
        away
                away
down the Iller
over the Alps
out to sea,
somewhere
where I can take
my dream of
a perfect world and
find the courage to
turn it
into reality.

AT THE UNIVERSITY
Letter from Hans, April 1939

Dear family,

Now that my term of Reichsarbeitsdienst
is over, I'm finally here,

soaking up everything from zoology
to Greek, botany to Nietzsche,

my thirst to learn all I can
remaining unquenchable.

Words of great philosophers
tumble into my ears

through my mind, whispering,
Knowledge is power.

I relish every moment here, despite knowing
that as soon as the semester ends,

knowledge won't matter,
at least not to the Reich.

Instead of our minds,
they merely want our young, able bodies,

carting us off to the fields of East Prussia
for voluntary farm work to feed our Volk.

Voluntary, they say, and yet,
we didn't volunteer.

OUR NEW FLAT

Vati's tax accounting business is
doing so well that he finds
us a new home, right
on the Münsterplatz in the
        center
of the city, opposite the
towering Münster itself.

We move in, delighted
by the most marvelous
home we've ever had,
even if it also means
that the ubiquitous
        flags
        parades
        fanfare
will be stopping right outside
our doors each
time crowds amass
to celebrate
whatever else this
Reich has done.

A SUMMER VISIT

Just like last summer, these
warm months mean
        sketching by the Iller
        picking berries with my siblings
        enjoying the frische Luft outdoors
but unlike last summer, this one
also means
        some snatched time with
            Fritz
        still very much a good friend
        and perhaps something more
as we both learn
what we're willing
to give, what we're willing
to take, in spite
of our differences.

Together we celebrate
the glory we can still find
around us
as this regime works so hard to strip
splendor from the world.

I escape
into the freshness
of the daisies Fritz gives me, wrap

an arm around his neck, press
my lips to his,
his mouth tasting
of freedom.

DRIVING LESSON

Nothing's happened at
any of Germany's borders
        yet, but
the mood in Ulm is
        tense, tight, wound up,
the sense that something's about
to blow ticking
in the background.

Fritz gets his father's car one
fine Sunday, and with Hans and
Werner miraculously at
home too, we four pile
in, head to the
Bodensee, its glittering
waters beckoning
us to dive in.

Cursed with the
curse of girls, all I can do is
watch, but once they're
done swimming,
I take the lead on
the way home, sitting
behind the steering
wheel, learning
everything
I need to know about

driving from my
teacher, ever-patient Fritz.

Someday soon
there might not be
any boys around
to do the driving.

WAR

My family and I huddle
around the radio,
the Führer's speech blaring
through the sitting room:

> Tonight for the first time
> Polish soldiers have fired
> shots upon our territory.
> Since 5:45 a.m.,
> return shots have been fired!
> From now on,
> bomb will be met by bomb!
>
> Whoever fights with poison
> will be fought back with poison.
> Whoever ignores the rules of warfare
> can expect the same
> from us.
>
> I will lead this struggle
>   as long as I need to
>   and how I need to
> until the security of the Reich
> has been guaranteed.

Faces pale
at the news that Germany
is now at war,

war that means

        Fritz
        Hans
        everyone

could be sent
to battle any day,
thanks to the Vaterland
pulling the strings.

FRONT AND HOME FRONT
Letter to Fritz, September 1939

Dear Fritz,

I got your
letter — danke schön!
I hope you receive
mine, although I'm not
sure what comfort
letters from
home will be
with the Blitzkrieg
and its

    bombs

    bullets

    artillery

striking around you.

Don't forget
all the innocent
people the Blitzkrieg
hurts.

You're probably thinking,
It's for the Vaterland,
but I'm sorry,
that's
no
excuse.

P.S.

Do they monitor
the mail
I send you?

RESPONSE

Fritz tells me
officers' mail
isn't
censored,

that I should
feel free
to say
what I like,

which is good
because I have
plenty
to say.

1940
Promises

While the Blitzkrieg
hammers, pounds, blasts
far to the east, we only notice
ripple effects
here at home.

We drink
the last of our tea, spread
the last of our jam
on dry fruitcake, but
rationing is nothing
compared with the shadow
of war pressing close.

I know
that boys I know
might die, but I can't let
them lose their souls
as well.

I take
each of my male friends
by the hand, make
each of them look
me in the eye, promise
never to fire his weapon
at the front.

Fritz doesn't understand
why this defiance matters
so much to me,
won't acknowledge
that our strongest weapon
is our refusal
to follow blindly.

Vati says nothing
but his smile
          my father's approval
when I stand up
for what's right
means the world.

TOY SOLDIERS

Fritz misunderstands
my opinion about
soldiers, the army, the war.

> Our opinions really aren't
> all that different.
> I feel that I must
> defend the side of the soldier,
> that I must
> defend the side of duty
> because duty is my daily life,
> but I want the same things as you:
> truth, justice, the greater good.

Wrong.
Regimes might change,
leaders might change,
orders might change,
but the profession of
a soldier is simple—
        obedience.

Soldiers must carry out
the orders they receive
whether they find
those orders
        good

or not,
and since I won't be with
Fritz in the field, all I can hope
is that his conscience might
remember
mine
when it matters
most.

LIFE AT THE REAR
Letter from Hans, May 1940

Dear family,

The sudden Blitzkrieg,
a drawn-out Sitzkrieg,

now our marching orders
and we move out,

leaving Germany behind
passing through Luxembourg, arriving in France —

the tail end of a gray Wehrmacht wave
of occupation.

Ordered to commandeer the best houses,
I'd feel more at home in the straw.

What are we, thieves?
Yet I'm one of them, like it or not.

We're twitchy, nervous, apprehensive,
the boredom and anxiety

at the rear
slowly driving me mad.

Not far away, artillery rumbles,
dark flak paints the sky,

the war a pot about to boil over,
as we wait, trapped inside.

SELFLESSNESS
Letter to Fritz, June 1940

Dear Fritz,

People shouldn't be
        ambivalent
about the world around
them simply because
everyone else
is ambivalent.

People who
        refuse
to open their eyes
are more than ambivalent —
they are guilty.

How can we expect
        justice
in this world
if we're not prepared to
sacrifice ourselves
for what's right?

DARK NIGHTS

Waking in the night,
I worry about
Fritz
training boys in the
      art of war
Hans
heading west with
the Wehrmacht
      into France
Werner
not far behind
following in
      their footsteps.

My boyfriend.
My brothers.

The three of
them are only a few drops in a
sea of soldiers
      soldiers who might die
      soldiers who might have to kill
and for what?

The walls of
my bedroom creep
toward me, stealing
my sleep for the rest
of the night.

THE FIELD HOSPITAL
Letter from Hans, July 1940

Dear family,

Casualties flow
thick as the muddy Somme

through the doors
to my hands.

Today I counted
twenty operations, two amputations.

I don't know how much longer
I can watch this butchery of ours.

TRUTH IN RUMORS

Before becoming
a mother, Mutti used
to care for the sick, and when her
nursing friends visit, the rest of
us at home make
ourselves scarce, not wanting
to hear tales of
        illnesses
        injuries
        hospitals.

But from where I sit
clear across the room today, nose in
a book, whispered words grab
my attention, all strung
together around
        disabled children
        vans
        poison gas
        murder.

Mutti's face goes
white and my ears ring
with horror.

Innocent children
killed
by this regime.

Yet what can anyone
        do
to stop it?

WOMEN'S WORK

Now that this ugly truth
has reached my ears, all hope
I once held
for a better world
dies.

Turning away
would be cowardly,
so I'm determined
to make my voice heard—
       to Fritz
       to my family
       to my friends
to anyone who'll listen.

Some people look
at me, smile, think
She's just a girl, but
Vati raised us to be
politically minded,
after all, and I'm not
about to forget
how I was
brought
up.

FATHERS AND SONS
Letter to Fritz, September 1940

Dear Fritz,

I'm happy to share
what I think
about the German Volk.

A soldier's oath
    to his Volk
    to his Führer
is like the unconditional
love of a son to his family.
Even if a father hurts someone,
his son backs him up.

But he shouldn't.

Justice
is more important
than family,
than Volk,
than Führer.

Justice
is more important
than anything.

CHANGES

Away from home for
practice teaching—
       a stint I hope will fulfill
       my labor service requirement
       for the Reich
       so I can finally move
       on to the university—
and everything feels
wrong.

This might be
a step closer to a future
that matters, but
I can't see how life
can go on like this at all,
as though nothing
around us has
changed in the slightest.

I carry out my duties, focusing
on the children here, but when
night falls, I dive
deep into my books,
my writing paper,
the arrival of the day's post.

Letters from my family slip
me snippets of home, while

mine to Hans and Fritz place
me in their back pockets
as they slice
their way west.

But I already know
nothing will ever
be the same again.

LOVE LETTER

Fritz's letter from Calais is
different from
his regular letters.

> Today I'm writing the hardest letter
> I've ever written you.

My throat tightens
as I read on to find lines
I never expected

> (though I should have,
> since I was the one who wanted
> the both of us to fly free).

Still, I don't need to hear

> about her big, dark eyes
> or her sad, dreamy smile.

I don't need to hear
how Fritz says he

> can't
> escape
> me

even as he lies
in another's arms.

I don't need him to apologize
for hurting me.

We've both made mistakes,
both tired of me pushing
him away as often as I draw him near.

I know I'm difficult, but with the world
the way it is, someone has
to be difficult.

I'll always love
Fritz, but I love
me more.

SOLITUDE
Letter to Fritz, October 1940

Dear Fritz,

Even when surrounded by
the most kindred
spirits, I sometimes crave
solitude.

Especially now, with so much
darkness closing in around us, being
alone is as important to me as
food and drink.

I hope you find
good friends
     wherever
you go, but
I hope you can brave
it alone, too.

THE END

FEBRUARY 18, 1943
Torture

Herr Mohr studies me
across the desk, as though
      the information I've been trying
      so valiantly to conceal sits
      printed across my face
or as though
      he can read
      my apprehension
      of what's yet to come.
Boom-boom,
boom-boom.

                    Is something bothering you,
                    Fräulein Scholl?

I decide to admit
the latter.
I've heard the Gestapo tortures
the accused for confessions.

                    Herr Mohr chuckles. *You're*
                      the victim
                    of misinformation. We
                    don't do that.

My eyes narrow. I don't know what
to believe, but if his words are
true, I deserve

proof that the same holds
true for Hans.
I'm worried about my brother.
I'd like to see him.

> *If that would satisfy you.* He
> gets to his feet, leaves
> the room, opens the
> door beyond.

In a room exactly like
mine, Hans turns
his head to meet my gaze and
the courage he sends
me matches the courage I send
him and relief floods
me when I realize
that in spite of the
evidence they gathered
at Hans's feet,
that in spite of my own
foolish actions,
we still have
a chance
to survive this.

INNOCENT

As abruptly as the door opened,
it closes once more, snuffing
out all light and air and
hope, leaving
Hans and me on
our own once again.

Stay alert,
I warn myself, *be careful,*
but it seems
Herr Mohr believes
my lies so far.

When he asks
if I touched
any of the leaflets scattered
around the halls,
I'm relieved to tell the truth.

When I saw a stack
of those leaflets
on the balustrade,
I couldn't help myself,
I couldn't stop myself.
I gave them a shove toward
the atrium below, but I realize now
it was a stupid thing to do.

I bow my head,
clasp my hands,
a picture of innocence.
*I regret it but
can't change it.*

Herr Mohr watches,
paces, stops, nods.

> *I understand, Fräulein Scholl.*
> *We've all done things*
> *we regret.*

Yet his questions
continue.

BEFORE

1941
Duty

The boys have
their duty as soldiers, but
my duties continue, too — no
matter how much I'd rather
        not
serve this Reich.

My attempt to replace
Reichsarbeitsdienst with
teacher training fails, and
the only way to study
at the university
is to give up
six months of my
life to the Führer.

KRAUCHENWIES

Reichsarbeitsdienst
at Krauchenwies labor
camp means
bone-chilling cold,
armies of mice scampering
across the floor,
endless days of
mindless tasks:
      6:00 a.m. wake-up
      calisthenics
      flag raising
      National Socialist songs
      ideology lessons
      work, work, work,
nothing
that requires
a brain.

At night: locked
up in the barracks
with ten other
girls
      chattering and giggling
like a flock of southbound
geese while I'm trying
to read and all
I want to do
is break

out of here toward
somewhere
I can make
a difference.

FEELINGS
Letter to Fritz, February 1941

Dear Fritz,

In spite of
everything, I know
I can always count
on you.

We don't need
        promises
        exclusivity
        a sure future.

Your words, your
love from afar make
me fonder
of you
than ever.

TRAPPED

Bad as it is to
be a cog in this
terrible machine,
the worst comes
today,
when we learn
we're to have
       six
       more
       months
in this straitjacket.

I'll never
       get out of here
never
       make a difference
never
       escape.

The war booms
on while I sit
here helpless, unable
to do anything to
stop it.

BIRTHDAY

I turn twenty at
Krauchenwies, surrounded
not by family and friends
but the same
group of girls who
        shatter
my reading time with
their incessant interruptions
every
night.

I don't even try
to celebrate.

THIS IS LOVE

Fritz marches east, part of
the next big invasion—
      the next big thundering
      storm cloud—
his words jumping
off the page.

I can almost feel
the scratchy wool
of his uniform
as though he's pressing
me to his chest, but
it suffocates
me as much as it comforts
me.

Though I can't imagine
the dangers people face
on all sides of this war daily,
Fritz's letter ignores
the horror, focuses on
me, responding to
my news of extended labor service.
His words empower
me as only he can:

You must follow
     your heart
     your mind
     your conscience
or you won't be
Sophie any longer.

In spite of everything that's come
between us,
no one
knows me
so well.

STUDENT LIFE
Letter from Hans, May 1941

Dear Sophie,

A bit of respite,
a bit of freedom

here at the university
after such a long wait.

Despite the constant drills
in the student company,

most of my time here is pleasant,
with lectures into the evenings,

excursions to the mountains,
glowing under the bright, blinding sun,

especially now
that it's truly spring.

Just think of how splendid it'll be
when you're finally here, too!

SERMON BY BISHOP AUGUST VON GALEN

Back at home from
labor service, and Hans is
here for a few
days too, in between his
l o n g   stretches
of time at
          the university and
          the front.

My big brother doesn't say
a word as he hands
me a letter, a printed
sermon
by a bishop:

I have been informed
that hospitals in Berlin are preparing
lists of inmates who are classified
as unproductive members
of the national community
and that these people are to be removed
from these establishments and killed.

German men and women!

Article 211 of the German Penal Code
is still in force, in these terms:
"Whoever kills a man with deliberate intent
is guilty of murder
and punishable with death."

LEAFLETS

The words steal
the breath
from my
lungs, trapping
the air in
my throat.

It's just
like Mutti's
friend said:
innocent people,
murdered.

But.
A response.
A condemnation.

This bishop, standing
up in the
face of
tyranny!

Someone has typed
up his sermon, duplicated it, sent
it to households across Germany.

A leaflet.
It's brilliant.

Leaflets like this can reach
individuals with a message
for the masses, can spread
the truth, can show
the world what's happening.

Leaflets like this might make
people act.

POLICE ORDER OF THE IDENTIFICATION OF JEWS
September 1941

Jews six years and older
are forbidden to appear
in public without
displaying a Jewish star.

The Jewish star should
consist of a yellow
Star of David on a black
background with the
inscription *Jude*.
It should be fixed
over the left breast
of all clothing.

This order goes into
effect in 14 days.

On behalf of the Interior Minister
Reinhard Heydrich

DISAPPEARANCES

Soon after Jews
are ordered
to wear stars, new
rumors circulate.

Jews from Ulm,
deported—
first to Stuttgart
then out of Germany
entirely.

Where
     are
          they
              being
                  sent?

WINTER RELIEF

It's that time of year again:
the collection drive for
> wool
> furs
> warm socks
to send to the soldiers at the front.

But my family and I are through
with this regime, through
with its Führer, through
with these attacks on innocent
countries, innocent people.

This
war
must
stop.

We'll give
nothing.
We'll do
nothing that will
help prolong
the war,
I tell Fritz.

He valiantly tries
to explain why help is
needed but soon recognizes
the futility of his efforts.

A PRAYER

Once again in the night,
worry and
despair and
hopelessness worm
their way through me, the walls
once again pressing
close, and
all I can do is pray
for the oppressed
  wherever they might be
for my brothers
  that they survive this war
for my faraway friends
  whose letters do
  nothing to bring
  us closer
for Fritz
  whom I hope to come to love,
  hard as it is some days
for my own soul
  desperate, hungering
  beyond measure, finding
  satisfaction only in nature:

the sky
the stars
the silent earth.

1942
Happy New Year

A handful of snowy days
in the mountains
       with Hans
       his girlfriend Traute
       our big sister Inge
       some other friends—
hoping the arrival of
1942 will bring
with it the change we all
so badly desire.

We ski, drink tea, sit
around the stove by candlelight,
our discussion focused
on these turbulent times.

We share
intellectual awakening,
but we're all too mired
in our own despair to know
what to do about it.

When the day's done, I turn
in to sleep, clinging
to hope that this
self-contained utopia might become
more than the dream it will feel like
when our holiday ends,

when I go back
to my next term
serving this Reich
I despise.

HOMESICK

Reichsarbeitsdienst in Blumberg,
and homesickness crashes
into me with ferocity, not
so much for home itself, but
for the feeling of
home.

It aches
to be so far away
from the life
I once knew,
from the life
I hope to lead,
from the life
everyone around
us deserves.

Like the winter relief
collection, my role working
for this Reich is part of what
allows this regime
to continue.

Each day I serve it
makes me want to fight it
all the more.

BEHIND CLOSED DOORS

After all these years
back and forth
on and off
hot and cold
something about
      the cozy inn
      the scent of fresh linens
      the knowledge that
            each time I see Fritz
            might be the last time
makes me toss
my jumbled thoughts out
the window.

I shut
the room's door, step
closer to Fritz, pull
him onto the bed.

MUTINY OR LOYALTY
Letter from Hans, February 1942

Dear family,

I'm a prisoner (again),
punished this time

with my entire unit
in the student company for mutiny.

I didn't do anything myself
(except refuse to name names),

but with one of my best friends
accused, I lose all respect for informers

stepping forward to denounce others
when we're interrogated separately.

The result is four weeks
confined to barracks, all of us,

when we — and certainly I — have
much more important things to do.

Still, nothing will divert my attention
from what really matters.

MY PURPOSE

Finally, I'm almost
done, after my months
in Krauchenwies and Blumberg,
but each day of Reichsarbeitsdienst
is one day less
of a life that matters.

Soon, very soon,
I'll be released, my path
to the university
finally clear,
where, God willing,
I'll find a way
to act.

DANGEROUS GAMES

I tingle as I sit
beside Fritz on the train,
our last chance to be
alone before I head
off to university and he returns
to the front.

We have a compartment to ourselves,
        a weekend to ourselves,
                the world to ourselves,
                        if only for a few days.

We open the window, let
the spring air inside, and it wraps
around us like a soft blanket, a rare
reminder of bygone days.

I find myself at
a crossroads with Fritz as he
goes to fight
for this regime I oppose, but
even if I don't know
what the future holds for
either of us, I know
I can trust
him with my secrets.

I need a favor—
some money and a voucher—
so I can get
a duplicating machine.

For a long moment,
Fritz pales, deflates, falters.

> *I can try.*
> The tremble in his
>   voice betrays him.
> *But you must be careful,*
>   *Sophie.*
> *Something like that*
>   *can cost*
> *you your head.*

For now, we let
the lovely breeze
carry us away.

BETWEEN THE LINES
Letter from Hans, March 1942

Dear family,

I wonder
if you received my last letter.

My own mail
is very irregular.

I sympathize with the Gestapo, spending hours
deciphering all the messy handwriting,

but duty is duty,
after all.

THE END

FEBRUARY 19, 1943
Denial

After an impossibly brief
sleep in a cell with
another female prisoner, I'm back
on my chair in front of Herr Mohr
      curtains drawn
      lamp bright
      walls close
once again mixing
a bit of truth with my lies.

           Fräulein Scholl, tell me again,
              at what time
           do you receive your
              mail each day?

In the morning
before we leave for class.

           Have you purchased any
           postage stamps
              recently? How
              many? Where?

Yes, I purchased perhaps ten or twenty
at the post office on Leopoldstraße.

He leans forward over the desk, steeples

his fingers, traps
me in his steely blue eyes.

> The Gestapo is well aware
> that someone has been
>   mailing
> treasonous leaflets like
>   these
> in Munich, in other cities.
> Tell me the truth.
> Were you involved?

I didn't have the slightest
thing to do with that.

SILENCED

A knock summons
Herr Mohr, who marches
out, returns
a moment later,
chin high, lips pursed,
triumphant.

> *Your brother has confessed.*
>   *We have*
> *the evidence from your flat.*

A chill passes
through my entire body,
like I've fallen
through thin pond ice,
the rushing water keeping
me submerged,
the mounting pressure keeping
me from finding
a way out.

I shudder, tremble, quake,
but I know what I must do, and I rise
up through the ice, chin raised.

> *I'd like to confess*
>   *as well.*

My words slice the air, freezing
Herr Mohr in place, draining
his cheeks of color.

The war for Germany
          is lost,
young lives
          sacrificed in vain.

My voice strong
as my resolve, I tell
how Hans and I
          came up with the leaflets last year,
          bought paper, envelopes, stencils, stamps,
          typed the addresses,
          delivered our message.

We intended
to stop the current regime
by reaching the
German Volk who feel
the same way and convincing
them to join us.

But it's not enough,
and Herr Mohr presses, insisting
we didn't do it alone.

Small lies crack
the surface of my confession
as I do my best to keep
the focus on
            us,
the suspicion off
            friends who were
            involved,
but in spite of myself
I've soon implicated
Alex as a helper, admitted
Traute and Willi knew
of our activities, confirmed
Herr Mohr's suspicions.

I pause then,
trying to suppress
the panic growing inside me,
hoping at the very least
that I've placed
            most
of the blame
            on my brother and me.

His face hard, his eyes harder,
Herr Mohr asks
if I have anything to add.

I did the best I could
for my country. I don't regret
what I did and accept
the consequences for my actions.

With these words
I finally
silence
Herr Mohr.

MY CONFESSION

Herr Mohr hands
me the confession they've typed
up, listing everything I've told
them, asks me to
              sign, leaving
the room to give
me time.

I read the words that make
me sound like an incredibly
brave girl, and I vow
to remain true to who
I am on paper, though the
chilling wave of dread rising
within me tells
a different story.
Boom-boom,
boom-boom.

There's no way
              out
of this cage.

BEFORE

1942
Early Birthday

After a fierce goodbye hug
from my parents, I balance
everything in my arms so I can board
the train to Munich:
        a suitcase with
                fresh laundry
                my most treasured books
                paper, envelopes, pens,
        a satchel with
                a bottle of wine
                a homemade birthday cake.

A whistle, and the train chugs,
puffs its way out of the station, and I lean
my head out the window to call
a last goodbye.

I'm about to turn
twenty-one, and
my future is
finally
about to begin.

MUNICH HAUPTBAHNHOF

With the train's last
mouthful of steam billowing
behind me into the sky,
my fingers twitch,
my heels bounce in anticipation.

Before the train has even
come to a halt, I jut my
head out the window, my
heart already bursting with glee.
　　　Hans!

I wave and
he waves back and
the train stops and
we run for each other and
hug and I almost can't believe
how happy I am
that I'm finally here.

MY ARRIVAL

I'm in love
with everything

and everyone and every
single moment spinning
past me
in bright swaths of color
here in Munich

now that I've
earned the right
to learn in a place
where I can
finally
make
a
difference.

THE ENGLISH GARDEN

My life becomes
discussions of literature in Hans's flat,
cheap dinners at sidewalk cafés,
walks to the English Garden
with
        books
        music
        friends,
our spirits light as dandelion fluff.

We all know
we'll be sent back
to serve the Reich soon enough,
but now that I'm here
to live and learn among
such fine minds, my eyes must
reflect the world and
all its brightness
back to them.

SUNSET

As if in a dream, the sun
i n c h e s
toward the horizon, sending
golden ripples of warmth and
joy through the trees towering
over us and sprinkling
our blanket with
droplets of light
as we lounge
on the sweet grass.

I wish
I'd brought
my sketchbook
along. If I had, I'd

draw Alex,
    half-Russian
    half-German
    fully charming, playing his balalaika,
    his pipe, his thoughtful expression,

his best friend, Christoph,
    young, melancholy, devoted
    to his wife, Herta, and
    their two small children,
    his eyes glowing moons
    when he speaks of them,

bright, assertive Traute,
      the current in Hans's long
      list of girlfriends that's sure
      to get longer.

Instead, I laze away,
imagining
their completed sketches
on paper as the five of us share
music, wine, stories,
while I take
in deep breaths
of rose-scented air, savoring
these singular moments, tucking
them in a deep
corner of my mind
far removed
from the harsh reality of
the outside world
and locking
them away to remind
myself that life like this
can exist.

RUMORS

As I settle into
my newfound freedom,
finding
      a place to live
taking
      my first classes
slipping
      beside Hans and his
      friends like a slim volume of
      poetry among their thick tomes
something shakes
me back to the ominous
darkness closing in around us.

Chilling rumors dart
from mouths to ears
about plans Herr Hitler is
carrying out, plans that have blown
up and expanded
and twisted, plans
that have become
reality to Jews in
Germany, in
Poland, and beyond:
      countless concentration camps
      unwanted resettlement
      systematic
      murder.

A PRAYER

Summer arrives
with a letter from Fritz,
in Russia leading
his unit east, and he shares
more details that make
all the rumors I've heard
undeniable.

It's shocking,
the way my commander
callously tells me of
        the slaughter of
        all the Jews in occupied Russia,
the way he matter-of-factly supports
        this behavior.

How happy I was
to return
        to my field cot
        to you
        to my prayers.

I say
a prayer too,
but I fear
our prayers
will do
nothing.

A LEAFLET

I'm standing
in the corridor during a
break between lectures
when Traute bursts
forward, thrusting
a paper at me.
> *Read this.*
> She whispers, stealing
> a glance over her shoulder.

I hold
the paper close, skim
the typewritten page, take
in its daring, fearless words.

Isn't it the case that
every honest German today is
> ashamed
of his government?

It's as though whoever wrote
this was reading
my mind.
Boom-boom,
boom-boom.

A leaflet—just like

the bishop's.
I read
more.

Carry out passive resistance —
       resistance —
wherever you are, impede
the atheistic war machine before
it's too late!

I read on and on, digesting
a passage by Schiller,
an author whose works sit
on our shelves at home, until I come
to words I recognize well, this
time by Goethe.

And the beautiful word of freedom is
whispered and stammered,
until in unfamiliar novelty we cry
from the steps of our temple
once again captivated:
Freedom! Freedom!

Traute and I stare
at each other while the lines
from this leaflet thunder

in my ears
though
we say nothing,
the silence echoing
through the hall.

THE FUTURE

The bell rings, Traute and I bid
each other farewell, I turn back
to the lecture hall, the truth sharp in my mind.

Hans started
this without
me.

Duplicating leaflets and sharing
them with the world —
this was my idea.

My own brother excluded
me, probably thinking,
She's only a girl.

And instead of me, he might
have brought someone else
into his confidence.

Certainly not Traute (another *girl*). Not
Christoph, not with his wife and
children. Maybe Alex?

Bitterness bubbles up inside me, but I can't
confront Hans now — not when he's leaving
for the front in a few weeks.

Not the time to talk
of a future
that might not happen.

INKY HANDS

The next time Hans comes
over, I almost say
something dozens of
times, but mostly I
observe
him with new eyes—
   my brother I already
   so admire,
   the center of the circle here,
   its sun—
and I'm already
less angry with him for doing
what I would have done myself
and instead I feel
proud,
especially when a glance
at his ink-stained fingers confirms
my suspicions.

Wear gloves
next time, I
silently beg.

ANOTHER LEAFLET

If I thought the first leaflet was
powerful, it's dwarfed by the
second, with its attack
on each and every
one of us.

My heart aches
as I read
details
      of the bestial
         murder of 300,000 Jews
      of the annihilation of the youth
         of the Polish aristocracy
accusations
      of
      the
      apathetic
      behavior
      of
      Germans.

Worse, when I read
      a German shouldn't only feel pity —
      no, much more: complicity
guilt washes over me
over what I've done
      and haven't done

and how I contributed to this
reign
of
terror
and I for one refuse
to be guilty
going forward.

A PROMISE

My resolve steadies
as I read the next leaflet's call for
>sabotage in armament plants,
>sabotage at all gatherings,
>sabotage in the areas of science and scholarship,
>sabotage in all publications.

The boys are about to leave
for the front, but I swear,
when Hans returns,
he won't be able to keep
me from his side.

WHITE ROSE

Another day, and
one more leaflet winds
its way into
my hands.

Breathless, I read
> Every word
> that comes out of Hitler's mouth
> is a lie.

While all of the leaflets are
dangerous, while all of them are
treasonous, this one is
more—pithy, sharp, aggressive.

My blood pulses
through my veins
as I read
> We *must* attack evil
> where it is strongest,
> and it is strongest
> in the power of Hitler.

The leaflet ends
with the most ironic
words of all:

The White Rose
will not leave you
in peace!

The White Rose is
the perfect name
for these efforts—
poetic, pure, full of mystique—
but the truth is
once the boys report
for duty, they'll be away
at the front, they'll be
leaving Munich
very much in peace.

Even though they must have spent
          hours
typing, duplicating, sending
these leaflets,
there won't be more after they leave.

Perhaps some of the recipients have made
more copies, sent them on, widening
the circle of the White Rose.

But many more have probably destroyed
the papers, too afraid to let
the ink stain their hands.

A LAST RESPITE

With time running
short, we all escape
to the mountains, invited
by Christoph's wife, Herta,
for the weekend.

Tucked away in their
home a world away from
Munich, it's easy to breathe,
easy to see
what still matters here:

>   the bubbly laughter
>   of children

>   the gentle kisses
>   of young lovers

>   the everlasting beauty
>   of the hills
>   the flowers
>   the sky

the things that
everyone
deserves.

AN APOLOGY

In Munich for only
one
more
week, I can't
stay silent any longer.
I know Hans is
leaving for the front, I *know*
he might not return,
and in case he doesn't,
I need him to know
that I know.

Leaflets in hand,
I present myself in the
atelier—a private space our new
friend Manfred offered
Hans for gatherings while he's
away on business.

With one glance
at me, Hans breaks,
dissolves, spills
the truth.

I'm sorry for not telling you.
It was Alex and me—
   no one else.
But we can do more
    together
if we make it back
alive.

I nod, we embrace, my fear
for his life eclipsing
all else.

ROBERT MOHR, GESTAPO INVESTIGATOR
June 1942

More envelopes
are turned in to the station:
addressed
to professors,
writers,
artists,
people typically sympathetic
to such weak, liberal ideas.

Leaflets
criticizing the Reich,
leaflets
calling for resistance,
leaflets
filled
with treason.

The hunt
for the masterminds
of this plot
begins.

THE END

FEBRUARY 20, 1943
A Golden Bridge

I have nothing
more to say,
Herr Mohr has nothing
more to ask,
and yet the next
time he summons
me, he throws
me a lifeline.

> *You can still save*
> *yourself, Fräulein*
> *Scholl.*

Boom-boom,
boom-boom.
A sliver of light enters
the room, and I'm certain
the entire world can hear
the pounding in my chest.

> *Tell me you were only*
> *following your older*
> *brother,*

> *and I'll recommend*
> *setting you free.*

My heart, beating
so confidently moments ago,
whimpers, withers, dies,
but my voice gathers
courage:
Nein.

ROBERT MOHR, GESTAPO INTERROGATOR

The girl's fate
is out of my hands.

She refuses
to betray her brother.
She refuses
to let me help her.

With her conviction,
her confession,
her brashness,
she has brought all of this
upon herself.

THE NEW PRISONER

When my cellmate, Else, tells
me they've captured
another member of the
White Rose, I stiffen,
frozen, waiting for the
verdict. Who?

> *You'll be glad to hear it's not*
> *the friend you were*
>   *worried about—*
> *Alex Schmorell?*

I press
my lips together, wait
for the blade to fall.
Boom-boom,
boom-boom.

> *It's someone you hadn't*
>   *mentioned.*
> *Someone named*
>   *Christoph Probst.*

Christoph?
        Christoph?
In an instant, I'm back
at his cozy home a few
months ago, surrounded

by his family—
         his *children*—
safe
from everything
except
fate.

Nein.

I turn
from Else, face
the wall, this news
a boulder attached
to my heart, dragging
me to the depths.

BEFORE

1942
The Farewell Party

I kiss each guest hello
> Traute
> Alex
> Christoph
> the boys' new friend Willi.

Not much later, Professor Huber—
> my favorite philosophy professor, whose
> lectures even medical students attend—
stops by.

It's meant to be
a lighthearted evening at
Manfred's atelier before
Hans and the others have to catch
an early-morning train
that will take them far
away to the eastern front
> and the death
> and destruction
> that awaits them there.

But the air crackles with fear
of the unknown
sizzling off the boys
burning their shadows
> into my mind,
and I hope

beyond hope that
they all return, especially
        Hans.

After the boys catch their train,
I'll be off to Ulm, with
nothing more
than the promise
of a bleak summer working
in an armaments factory,
but I know I'm lucky
my summer also holds
        the sanctuary of home
        no danger of losing my skin—
my dread channeled instead
        toward the lives
        of others.

But first, tonight.

I open bottles of wine and breathe
in conversations and freeze
time in moments, capturing
        each gesture
        each glance
        each grin
cataloguing
them in my heart.

MANFRED'S TRIP

As if the mood couldn't
get darker, Manfred shares
gruesome details
from his latest trip to Poland.

My skin grows
cold as he recounts
how squads of deadly SS Einsatzgruppen
     marched in
     rounded people up
     smashed rifle butts against bone
     left behind pits heaped high
     with layers of Jewish bodies.

Hans and I share
a glance as
images I cannot un-imagine
fill my mind with
horror.

I catch a similar glance
between Alex
     assigned to the same unit as Hans
and Christoph
     assigned to a unit near home to be close
     to his young family.

Christoph and I are staying
      here,
Hans and Alex are going
      there.

The silence
shrouding the room
overwhelms.

SAVING LIVES

When conversation gradually starts
up again, the boys turn
their attention to the weapons
they'll carry to the front, to the question
Will you fire them
or not?

Willi, the only one
who's already spent
time on the eastern front, raises
his eyebrows, glancing
at the others.
He says nothing.

> *If I have to,*
> Hans whispers,
> *in defense.*

But Alex shakes
his head.
> *I'm half-Russian and won't shoot Germans,*
> *half-German and can't shoot Russians.*

I take comfort knowing
that at least someone refuses
to be part of this madness.

Even one less bullet
can mean
one more life.

EXPECTATIONS

Over empty wine bottles, discarded
glasses without a drop remaining,
the last conversations lower
to a melodious hum
between
        Manfred and me
        Christoph and Alex
        Professor Huber and Hans.

With the sendoff almost
over, all I can hope
is that we'll have a reunion
some months down the road.

His eyes wide and bright, Hans shakes
Professor Huber's hand,
Christoph blinks furiously like he's willing
back tears, whispers
earnest thoughts to Alex.

Manfred bends
toward me as I help him return
the studio to order.
        You must write them
        cheerful letters while they're away.
        They'll see terrible
        things in the east.

I nod, remembering
Fritz's latest letter, hoping
Hans won't have
similar experiences, praying
this madness might come
to an end.

Manfred's lips press
together in a grim line,
his unspoken words hanging
in the air
like rain clouds.

I close my eyes and pray
that the world will
somehow change.

But I know it isn't
going to change
on its own, so I know
I must pray
for the courage to
bring it about.

THE WARSAW GHETTO
Letter from Hans, July 1942

Dear family,

After the long journey
through Germany and Poland,

Alex, Willi, and I clump together,
ambling through Warsaw

in train-crumpled uniforms,
trying to s t r e t c h our legs.

We share cigarettes,
coughing not when the smoke

enters our lungs,
but when we stub them out

and breathe in the polluted city air
that seems to grow thicker around the ghetto,

where the situation is just
as we've been informed.

What's happening here
makes me sick to my stomach.

THE ARMAMENT FACTORY

Back in Ulm
after the boys leave,
I carry out
my despicable duties at the
armament factory,
trying to be grateful
for the life I lead here
far away from the pummeling,
punishing hammer of artillery
that I pray doesn't reach
>>> Hans or
>>> Fritz or
>>> the others.

I might not be brave
enough for actual sabotage,
but I work painstakingly slow,
manufacturing as few
arms as I can.

THE VAST LANDSCAPE
Letter from Hans, August 1942

Dear family,

Russia is a giant church
with an infinite sky for a roof,

the music of thunderous artillery
resounding through the air, its organ.

Werner and I take long walks
in the countryside —

    what a miracle he's stationed
    only a few kilometers away! —

we all trade schnapps and stories and songs
make friends with daughters of local farmers

and Alex and I share cigarettes
with Russian prisoners

until those in charge slap
our wrists for being kind.

We shake our heads,
objecting to the lack of humanity,

but here it's hard to find
any humanity at all.

DUPLICATION

Away from Munich,
one thing is
       clear.

I'm sure Hans can use
a second
duplicating
machine.

I must ask
Fritz again
for some money.

VATI'S TRIAL

Almost as soon as I return
home, Vati's hauled
into court, where he's sentenced
to four months in prison
for calling Herr Hitler
a scourge of God
in his office.

It's a name
Vati's been calling
the Führer
for years.

But this time
his secretary
overheard.

FACTORY LIFE
Letter to Fritz, August 1942

Dear Fritz,

Vati's cornered
in prison while I sit,
helpless,
in front of the
    same machine
doing the
    same tasks
day after day
in the armament factory.

My soul aches.

MUTTI'S PLAN

After Vati's trial, Mutti frets,
       despondent,
but only for a day. She writes
the boys with a plan:

       Vati's been sentenced,
       you and Werner
       must write appeals for clemency.
       Bitte, Hans.
       Support from soldiers on the front
       could help reduce Vati's sentence.

I give Mutti a hug—
       all the support I can offer—
knowing that Hans's pride
will never allow
him to plead
for mercy.

SUFFERING AND SURVIVAL
Letter from Hans, August 1942

Dear family,

Vati's imprisonment starts today.
I'm so sorry for him, and for you,

but writing an appeal for clemency
is impossible. I won't beg. I just can't.

It'll be hard for Vati at first — as I know
all too well — but he'll only become stronger.

Today Alex and I came across
a Russian body

no one had bothered to bury,
and the only thing we could do

was to give him peace
under his own soil.

His head
was detached,

his body
crawling with worms,

his heart
bled into the earth below

one with his homeland
forever.

ROBERT MOHR, GESTAPO INVESTIGATOR
August 1942

After such progress
in the investigation
during the summer,
the trail has gone cold.

No new leaflets,
no new envelopes,
no new evidence
of treason.

I'm back at my desk,
pacing, fidgeting, twitching,
waiting
for the phone
to ring.

HUMANS AND MONSTERS
Letter to Fritz, August 1942

Dear Fritz,

After another endless
day carrying out soulless
duties hunched
over armaments
in the factory, sitting
next to a Russian worker
    imported to make weapons
      to use against her countrymen,
all I want to do
is scream.

The poor girl doesn't even understand
the things the overseers order
her to do, responding with the same
smile as always.

In rare moments of peace, I sneak
her snacks and she and I swap
vocabulary, demonstrating to
my German coworkers
that Russians are human beings, too.

So many women in front
of so many machines reminds
me of slavery, except

most of the German women
willingly chose
their own slave driver.

VISITING HOURS

I come home after
work at the factory for
a simple supper
with
        Mutti
        Inge
        Liesl.

Almost half our chairs
here at home stand
empty, waiting for
        Vati
        Hans
        Werner.

Once we wash
up the dishes, I grab
my flute, stand
on the sidewalk
as near as I can get to the
walls of Vati's cell and play
a tune I hope
will lighten his soul:
        The thoughts are free.

If Vati hears it, he'll know
the message
is meant for him.

THANK YOU
Letter to Fritz, August 1942

Dear Fritz,

Danke for sending
me the money!

It will most definitely
be put to good use.

INTERMISSION

At home, I sit
at the piano, play the same Bach piece
I once practiced daily, stumbling
through the music like
I'm once again learning
to walk, feeling
each key·
under my fingers,
each note
in my soul
      light
      airy
      profound.

Until Mutti breaks
my musical trance, clutches
the paper to her chest, says,
    Ach, nein! Not Ernst Reden!
and I'm frozen, knowing
another of our friends
has fallen,
    killed
by this senseless war.

DEAD BOYS AND GIRLS

I get
to my feet, stand
at the window waiting
to be overwhelmed
with feelings
and yet
when
a single
tear slips
out of my eye
and rolls down my
cheek, I feel
nothing
at all.

DECIDED

I turn
to the room, wipe
that single tear
away,
say,
That's it.
I'm going
to do
something
about this.

ACTION

I go
to a friend's for lunch, look
over my shoulder,
         pause,
pull eighty Reichsmark
from my pocket, pass
it across the table to him.

This high school boy—Hans—
is the younger brother
of another friend
and he looks
         naïve
         eager
         skittish
as he pockets the money.

                    His voice squeaks
                    but he says,
                    *I'll let you know
                    when I have it.*

THE FUTURE

With the boys still away
  my fear for their lives
    mounting
  every single night
my own long days
at the mind-numbing factory
in Ulm are crawling
to an end, like they are
for Vati,
who is soon—finally—
to be released.

This regime and
my shameful
complicity
in it make
me sicker every day,
and all I want to do
is stop,
do the right thing,
atone
for my actions.

Soon I'll be back in Munich,
where I can convince
Hans I'm ready to do more
and I won't
take no for an answer.

OMINOUS AUTUMN
Letter from Hans, October 1942

Dear family,

Today I received your news
that Vati's to be released early,

and my thoughts are with you all.
I can't wait to be home — just two more weeks.

I hope I'll see Werner
one last time before I leave.

At least we've been able to spend time
together here.

It's fully fall now, and my frosty breath
mingles with cigarette smoke,

hanging over me like a cloud.
Soon it'll be winter.

ULM HAUPTBAHNHOF

Chug, chug, screech.

The boys poke
their heads out the train's door, spot
me on the platform, burst
into smiles.

Hans! Alex!
They've come
back, windswept and disheveled,
but alive.
Warm, smelling like
      wet wool,
      caked-on mud,
      traces of sweat,
they wrap
strong arms around
me, around
each other, around
home.

Tonight
we'll have wine
and sing
and talk
      and breathe
until the sun comes up.

THE BREADWINNER
Letter to Fritz, November 1942

Dear Fritz,

Though Vati is home now,
today he was informed
he can no longer work
as a tax accountant.

We expected this after
his court sentence, but
it'll still make
things quite difficult for us.
Even if he finds
some bookkeeping work,
it won't pay as well,
so we might not be able to keep
the flat on the Münsterplatz.

Danke for offering
to help — we'll need it. But for now,
I'd be most grateful if you could
send me a package of envelopes.

ARRIVAL IN MUNICH

When we return to Munich,
Hans reminds me of me when I
was here the first time, falling
into this circle of
  friends
  smiles
  camaraderie
at the safe haven of
  the university's halls
  lectures
  labs.

He even falls
in love, this time with
  my friend Gisela
  (already replacing Traute, now a friend)
all of this in spite of the world crumbling
to bits around us.

I wish I could be
so light of heart, but
with everything I now know,
I'm ready to do whatever I can
to turn the German tide
against itself.

FRANZ-JOSEF-STRASSE

In the new flat I'm sharing
with Hans, I corner him, tell
him what's been worming
through my mind since he left
for the front.

I have ideas, plans, ways
we can share our views
> *with the university*
> *the city*
> *our country*
> *the world.*
I can't wait any longer.

Cheeks pale, his lips
a thin line, Hans nods.
> *I knew*
> *you'd want to help*
> > *right away.*
> A pause.
> *I'm sorry again I didn't*
> > *tell you*
> *in the summer.*
> *I was only trying*
> *to protect you.*

Danke.
I raise my chin.
But I don't need
anyone's protection.

TOO YOUNG

The next time I'm in Ulm, I find
out from young Hans
that he indeed procured
a duplicating machine with
the money I gave him.

But someone he thought
was a trusted friend informed
            the Gestapo
so Hans did the only thing he could
before it was too late:
he took the machine
to the Schiller Bridge, threw
it in the Danube, drowning
my hopes along
with it.

ALEX AND CHRISTOPH

Back in Munich, and Alex brings
Christoph by to visit,
and his face is long, his eyes
tremendously sad.

> Christoph tells
> us the same thing I told
> Hans:
> *I need to* do *something.*

We all agree we can't endanger
Christoph, not with Herta and their
young children at home—
           especially not with
           the family's third baby on the way—
but Hans of course sparks
to life, challenging
Christoph with something less risky:
drafting a leaflet.

> *Something that can*
> *open people's eyes.*
> *Something that shows*
> *Germans*
> *that losing to the Allies*
> *could be the best thing*
> *for Germany.*

Christoph pulls
his pipe from his pocket, goes
back to sit beside Alex, takes
a pinch of tobacco from his pouch.
Hans follows,
lights a match,
its flame
sizzling to life.

Drawing in a deep breath
of thick, smoky air,
Christoph nods, his eyes no longer
sad but whirring
with new purpose.

THE REAL ME
Letter to Fritz, November 1942

Dear Fritz,

I have a
     request
     confession
     prayer.

I haven't told anyone
else about this, but I know
you'll understand.

I'm filled with
fear
and nothing but
fear
and all I want
is for something
to take
this fear
away.

Please think of me
in your prayers.
You're forever
in mine, too.

SUPPLIES

To prepare
for our next leaflet mailing,
I take it upon myself to head
to the post office
on Ludwigstraße,
where the clerk eyes
me with suspicion
      making me eye
      the door
as he hands
me the one hundred stamps
I request.

Next time,
smaller amounts,
more
post offices.

At the stationery store,
      a stack of envelopes
      a pile of paper
      ink
      for the machine.

Whenever the boys are
ready, we'll have
all the materials
we need.

ROBERT MOHR, GESTAPO INVESTIGATOR
December 1942

After months of inactivity,
a clerk at the post office
on Ludwigstraße
has reported
something suspicious:

a
young
woman
buying
one hundred
stamps all at once.

A young woman:
not what I expected
at all.

This
manhunt
is
picking
up
speed.

DAY ZERO

FEBRUARY 18, 1943
The Suitcase

After another
late-night meeting with
      Hans
      Alex
      Willi
I sleep in, skipping
my morning lecture and letting
the diluted February sun kiss
me awake through the window.

I hear Hans rummaging
in his desk across the flat,
and I rub my eyes, wondering
if last night's talk
was just talk
or if
he's ready
to carry this out.

I'm up.

I splash
water on my face, get
dressed, run
a comb through my hair, make
some toast—
      the most normal things
      in the world—

and when Hans emerges,
      cheeks pale,
      pupils wide,
I ask
him about the suitcase
under the bed.

DOING SOMETHING

A smile filled
with recklessness spreads
across my brother's face,
and I can't help
grinning back, though
if I'm honest with myself
my insides are equal
parts
       dread
       and
       excitement.

I nod,
fingers trembling
with a rush of anticipation,
when I realize
he and I are really
going to do this.

THE UNIVERSITY

We pull on our coats, wind
our scarves around
our necks like nooses, pick
up the briefcase,
the suitcase, and step
outside into Franz-Josef-Strasse.

The sun that woke
me so gently now blinds
me, painting
the street with harsh strokes.

I stop, squinting,
before following
Hans down the block
toward the university.

WILLI AND TRAUTE

Blood pumping,
chests heaving,
Hans and I arrive
at the main doors of
the university just as
Willi and Traute tumble
outside, ten minutes
before the lecture ends.

For a moment,
the four of us stare
at one another,
breathless.

NO TURNING BACK

Their eyes popping wide,
Willi and Traute freeze,
taking in the two of us arriving
near the end of the lecture,
carrying
      the suitcase
      Hans's briefcase.

We exchange
a greeting,
but my brother and I
have a job to do.

With a meaningful nod
to our friends, we turn
to the door, Hans holds
it open for me, and I lead
the way inside.

PAPER SOLDIERS

We pass
through the main doors, head
upstairs to the corridors surrounding
the lecture halls, set
the suitcase on the ground,
open it.

Hans nods at me, watches
me reach in, pull
out a stack of leaflets.

He grabs
another thick fistful from
his briefcase, places them
        strategically
down one end of
the deserted corridor,
like a soldier
        setting up machine guns.

HURRY

Boom-boom,
boom-boom,
my heartbeat
pounds,
my heels
thunder
as I race
down the corridor,
where I place
small stacks
of thin papers
on the floor
beside each
lecture hall door,
where they
will be
impossible
to miss.

ESCAPE

Briefcase empty, Hans heads
for the back door, bursts
outside, spins
around, wild joy spreading

across his face until I catch
up, lift the suitcase,
wrinkle
my forehead in a frown.

> *There are still some left.*
> My words hang
> in the air like flak, shocking
> us both for a moment.

Let's go back in.
Hans leads
the way through the doors,
the air inside now oppressive.

FINISHING THE JOB

I follow
Hans back inside
toward the lecture halls
once again.

Our footsteps sound
more urgent now
as we hurry
up the marble steps
to the third floor, open
the suitcase once more, place
the last stacks of leaflets
on the balustrade.

We exhale,
sharing
a relieved smile.
Finished.

RELEASE

The suitcase should feel
light in my hands,
but now that it's finally
empty, its weight is
heavy as stones.

Hans heads
for the stairs, leather briefcase limp
at his side, and I follow,
our footsteps as innocent
as any
good
German
student.

We've done
so much today—
more than we've ever dared—
and yet,
the stack of papers on
the balustrade whispers
to me
           More.

I rest
my hand on it, the paper
sacred as a Bible.
I breathe, give

the stack a gentle push, and step
back to listen
to the papers fluttering
down to the ground
like a swarm of butterflies.

BEFORE

1943
The Beginning of the End

Just after we slide
into 1943, the news coming
out of Stalingrad
      of a losing battle the Führer's not willing
      to concede
shows how drastically the tide's turning
against this Vaterland.

Over breakfast, Hans and I stare,
      shocked
      saddened
      outraged.

*This can't
go on. We're going to lose
an entire generation.*
My voice breaks.
Behind my words,
terrible fear for Werner, Fritz,
other boys still there.

           You're right. Hans nods, sighs,
           pauses. *I'm going to
              draft a new
           leaflet, ask the others
              to do*

the same. Then we'll
  invite
everyone over to make
  plans.

WARTIME WISHES
Letter to Fritz, January 1943

Dear Fritz,

I'm following the news, filled
with worry since I know
you're near Stalingrad. I hope
you're not caught up in
the horrors
of this war.
I visit you so often
in my thoughts that
I sometimes feel
like you're close enough to touch,
and just in case, I whisper
into the void,
stay strong, stay good.

Wishing you
a hard spirit
and a gentle heart!

A NEW DRAFT

A shiver races
down my spine as I read
the beginning of Hans's new draft.

> The war is nearing
> its inevitable end.

These matter-of-fact words will
surely wake
Germany from its slumber.

> Hitler cannot win
> the war, only prolong it.

I nod, energized
by these lines, energized
to *do* something more to
somehow save
the boys I love
far away on the eastern front.

I picture them
     freezing
     shivering
     holding the line
and for what?

With winter about to grip
German throats with full force,
Russian troops closing
in like the jaws of a giant
trap, supplies running
as low as morale,
it's time to bring
these boys home.

We must speak
our minds—
we, the youth
of this terrible Reich,
our voices rising
in protest.

Hans meets
my gaze, his expression
resolute, making
me proud we're in
this together.

A MORAL OBLIGATION

Waiting for the others to arrive,
I remember the first
leaflets Hans and Alex wrote
back in the summer, with their
call to an elite slice
of the population, asking
educated readers to use their intellect
to make a stand.

Those leaflets had seemed so
wise to me back
then, but maybe they weren't
what was needed to mobilize
this Volk.

Now that we understand
how much deeper this threat goes —
our own soldiers
          freezing on the eastern front,
Russian peasants
          watching their homeland destroyed,
entire swaths of young Polish nobility ruthlessly
          murdered,
the Jewish inhabitants of the Warsaw ghetto,
          carted away on transports
          heavy as hearses —
we have a duty to share
the truth with the masses.

Attacks on freedom
can be countered by appealing
        to intellect.

Attacks on people
must be countered by appealing
        to morality.

I can only hope
all morals aren't
already lost.

THE GATHERING

Hans greets Willi at the door,
leads him inside,
and that's everyone—
the rest of us are already here:
Alex, Professor Huber, me.

Everyone's talking
about the professor's lecture on
the poet Heinrich Heine,
   censored
      for being Jewish,
   denounced
      by the Party
      as a degenerate,
  lauded
      by the professor
      for his brilliance.

I might not say
much, but I vow to fight
back
   with action,
      action,
       action.

DISSENT

Warmed up and ready,
the professor and the boys turn
to the next leaflet, locking
wits over philosophical differences
in the drafts Hans and Alex present.

Far too communist.
The professor shakes
*   his head.*
Especially Alex's draft.
One can be anti-Hitler
*   without*
leaning so far to the
*   left.*
You might find that
*   conservatives*
agree with you, but not
if you alienate
them completely.

Hans doesn't deny
the merit in the professor's arguments,
but my brother is
passionate in his own convictions,
and I fully agree
with him.

I press
my lips together, hoping
the professor will
give in.

Instead, he shakes
his head, finishes
his wine, bids
us farewell.

ROBERT MOHR, GESTAPO INVESTIGATOR
January 1943

After the stamps,
nothing.
No new envelopes
turned in,
no new leaflets.

Perhaps the recipients
are doing as the White Rose
asked and passing them on
instead
of turning them in.

It's time to step up
patrols, especially
at night.

PERVITIN WACHHALTEMITTEL

We're in for a l o n g night at
the flat, where we've set
up all the supplies, ready
to be put to use.

We man our battle stations. From
his pocket, Hans pulls out
some Pervitin—
       pills meant to keep soldiers
       awake at the front—
and the slim roll winds its way
around the room, ending
up in front of me.

Each of the boys pops
one without a second
thought, without missing
a beat of their work, but I had
no Pervitin at the factory, so I study
the small white tablet that falls
into my palm for
       several
       seconds
before placing
it on my tongue, holy
as a Communion wafer.

Within minutes, I feel
like I can do
anything.

A LONG NIGHT

All night long, my body tingles,
my fingers fly
as we duplicate
the leaflet, stuff
copies into envelopes, work
out the plan.

Alex and I will carry
suitcases full of them to
other cities and send
them from there.
We'll use local
         instead of long-distance stamps.
We'll give the appearance
         of a larger organization.

Yes, yes, yes.

We're prepared to paper
this Reich with a call to action, and
I've never been so ready
for anything in my life.

JITTERS

The day of my first trip dawns
with a great, gaping hole
of anxiety gnawing
at my insides.

Yet my fear
of doing nothing
is greater.

ON THE TRAIN

I board the train, set
the rucksack on the shelf
in one compartment, glance
over my shoulder, move
to sit in the next one.

Boom-boom,
boom-boom.

Out the window, soldiers patrol
the station, one will board
the train as usual, looking
for anything suspicious.

Boom-boom,
boom-boom.

The four walls cage
me in as I prepare
myself to deny
everything.

It takes an hour for the first
leg of my journey, but the contents
of the rucksack
in the neighboring compartment
      heavy
        with a thousand

envelopes
filled
with treason
make each minute stretch
into days.

FIRST STOP

I hop off the train
in Augsburg to mail
the first few hundred
leaflets.

I buy stamps, fix
them on the envelopes,
slip them into the mailbox.

When the next train rolls
in, I'm ready for
the next stop:
Ulm.

ANOTHER CHANCE

When I arrive
in Ulm, I dash into
the neighboring compartment
for the rucksack, hustle
off the train.

It's strange to be
here — *home* — with
           no plans
to see my family today.

Instead, I have
           firm plans
to give young Hans
one
more
chance.

He meets
me as appointed, shakes
my hand with a clammy
palm, accepts
the mountain of
2,500 leaflets I present
him.

I carefully instruct
him to address and mail

them from elsewhere, do
everything to keep our
families from suspicion.

He nods,
twitches,
nods again.

It'd be hard to
say who's more
nervous, but
       no one
will ever truly know,
since I hold
all my nervousness
deep inside.

TWO DAYS LATER

Another trip, this time to
Stuttgart. Even farther
than Ulm, it'll be
three
long
hours
on the train, with more
            stops, more
            soldiers, more
            chances for
            discovery.

Boom-boom,
boom-boom.

I press
my back against the
seat, try to ignore
the tightness down
my neck, do my best
to remember
to breathe.

SECRETS

I carry out the plan, send
all the leaflets, make
it back to Munich safely.

Still, secrets burn
my throat raw
with their desire
to escape.

Secrets about our work,
hidden truths I must bury
deep inside,
secrets I can't share
with the rest of my family
best friends from childhood
        even Fritz.

In the farthest reaches
of my mind lie
more secrets,
secrets of my own
        past
        guilty
        role
in this terrible
regime.

LIFE AND DEATH

I've fallen
asleep in the middle of the
afternoon only to wake
when a soft voice rises
up from across the flat.

Stalingrad!
Two hundred thousand
German brothers
sacrificed
for the prestige
of a military con man.

I rub
my eyes, get
to my feet, stumble
across the hall.

Christoph and Hans huddle
over a paper,
look up with a start, relax
when they see me.

Hallo, Sophie.

Good news! Christoph hands
the paper to Hans,
bursts

into a smile. *Herta had*
the baby.
A girl this time.

Congratulations! I cross
the room, give
him a warm hug.

I should be going. I hope
you like the draft. He
nods at Hans.

We'll see. Hans pockets
the paper. *We'll see.*

LEFT BEHIND

That night Alex and Willi come
by with a suitcase, and I can see
from the way Alex carries it that
it's not empty.

Before I can tell
them I want to come
along on their mission,
Hans turns
away from me, claps
Willi on the back, sneaks
something heavy, metallic
from his desk
into his coat pocket—
          his pistol?

I'm coming with you. I get
to my feet, move
for my coat, but
they're already heading
for the door.

                    *Not this time. Some things
                    are too dangerous
                    for you.*
                    Hans smiles, steps
                    outside.
                    Don't wait up.

In spite of
everything
I've done, my
big brother still thinks
I'm nothing
more
than a little
girl.

A VISIT FROM ULM

A few days later our
sister's visit eases
the tension in the air
at least a tiny bit.

Liesl is
soft-spoken,
calming, kind, and she lightens
the mood with tales of
Mutti, Vati, and
a neighbor's new baby, sweet
as marmalade from home.

With a contented smile,
Liesl breezes around
the flat, and for the briefest
of moments I float, suspended
above the both of us—
      me, in grave danger for my work,
      her, blissfully ignorant
      but safe and secure—
and I imagine
switching places with her.

But now that I know what
Germany has done, what
Germany is doing,
I'll never return

to being the girl I was
all those years ago.
My desire to do something
        to do the right thing
pushes all else aside.

I swoop
back into my own head,
all the more convinced
that the risky road
is the one
I must take.

ARMED FORCES REPORT

That afternoon we gather
in our small sitting room
before the radio broadcast:
        Hans, Liesl, and me
ready to find out what's happening
to our army in Russia.

The daily OKW Bericht begins
with the sound of horns,
drums, more music.

Each deep note from
the glorious fanfare strikes
familiar. They played
this music before one of
the previous reports.
Bruckner? Brahms?

               Across the room, Hans frowns.
               Liszt.
               Les Préludes.
               Remember?

The last time they played
this glorious piece was when Germany invaded
Russia, but there can't be any kind of
glory today. The last report revealed
Germany's Sixth Army

fighting the enemy on all sides,
nowhere near victory.

We wait, anxious
for the latest announcement.
The music stops.

> *The fight for Stalingrad*
> *is over.*

VICTORY AND DEFEAT

Over? My breath catches
in my throat. Is it true?
Have we actually, finally lost?

Hans and I glance
at each other,
eyebrows raised.

What does this mean?
Who's the victor?

They refuse
to admit we've lost,
but the last words
of the broadcast crash
over me with the ugly truth:
> *They died,*
> *so that Germany may live.*

Our soldiers
at Stalingrad,
dead.

HOPELESSNESS

I try to remember
the last words I wrote Fritz,
our last visit, last kiss,
but when I close
my eyes I can only picture
the once formidable German net unraveling,
the frozen Russian landscape
smoldering
in destruction, the lives
of those soldiers still there wasted,
and for nothing at all
in the end.

I hurry to find
his most recent letter.

> The situation here is hopeless.
> Unless I'm saved by some miracle
> or killed outright, the only other outcome
> I can imagine is Russian imprisonment.

A frosty wind whips
around me, across
an imagined tundra,
and the icy air bites
at my flesh, swallowing
me whole.

NIGHT MISSION

The broadcast ends, we digest
the news, thick and
hard to swallow as
gristle.

When Alex stops
by later Hans gets
to his feet, announces
their plan to do some work
in the clinic, but
the look he shares
with Alex tells
me they aren't planning
to go to the clinic at all.

Alex doesn't carry
a suitcase full of leaflets, but
instead Hans slips
on his coat, slides
some tools into
his pocket
      a can of tar
      thick brushes,
and I know
what they aim
to do.

Of course, with
Liesl here I can't
even beg
to come along—
not out loud, at least.

FRESH AIR

My lips purse,
my eyes narrow,
my glance
the only way I can
share my message:
Take me with you.

When Hans and Alex leave
anyway, I let
Liesl's calming voice distract
me from missing
out on the thrill of
danger in the dark.

She talks about
Fritz, Werner, others we know
at the front, but I only see
boys who might now be
dead, littered over the frozen earth
like rusted tin soldiers.

There is so much I want
to say, but the only words
I can muster betray
my need to escape

these
four
walls:
Why don't we go outside for
some frische Luft?

DOWN WITH HITLER

Outside with Liesl, armed
with the cover of darkness, I stop
at a freshly whitewashed wall, running
my hand over the perfect canvas,
whispering *Nieder mit Hitler,* tracing
the invisible words with my finger.

> Liesl goes pale, scans
> the street, skittish
> as a mouse.
> *Talk like that is*
>   *dangerous.*
> Her whisper shatters
> the quiet around us
> like a gunshot.

A thrill passes
through me as I glance
at the shadows
around us.
The night
is the friend
of the free.

THE MOST BEAUTIFUL ARTWORK

The next morning, when we head
down Ludwigstraße toward
the university, washerwomen scrub
> the walls
> the sidewalks
> the advertising posts
clear using wire brushes, trying
to hide the words that still remain
thick as the tar
they were painted with:
> *Freedom!*
> *Down with Hitler!*

We admire
the artwork as we pass,
Hans's raised eyebrows
the perfect picture
of innocence.

DAY ZERO

FEBRUARY 18, 1943
Jakob Schmid, Custodian

Like white doves,
gliding through the air
from above.

Was ist das?

Sheets and sheets
of paper.
I pick one up.
These words are treason.

My blood thunders,
choking
me in place
as footsteps
reach my ears
from three floors up,
from two figures
striding away,
alone.
Halt!

PAPER SNOW

The bell rings
and in perfect synchrony
the lecture hall doors swing
open, students stream
out, like dancers
in an elaborately choreographed
production, sweeping
down both sides of the staircase
toward the papers falling
to the ground.

My feet freeze
in place, my gaze surveying
the atrium, taking in
the area littered with leaflets picked
up by students, professors, everyone —
being carefully read.

Already I feel
like we've won.

JAKOB SCHMID, CUSTODIAN

Chest heaving,
I rush
three long flights
past others exiting
the lecture halls.

A boy and a girl.
Students.

Halt!

I take the boy
by the arm, and then the girl.

You
are
under
arrest.

CAPTURED

The custodian grips
our arms, leads
us to his superior's office, calls
the Gestapo, and
the two of them glare
at us, eyes narrow,
arms crossed.

It all feels like a dream:
      familiar
      expected
      inevitable.

They take
the suitcase,
the briefcase,
and I'm relieved
there's nothing else
for them to take.

ROBERT MOHR, GESTAPO INVESTIGATOR

The telephone rings,
and I answer,
Robert Mohr,
expecting usual daily minutiae
only to learn
that the custodian at the university
has apprehended two persons
suspected
of distributing
treasonous leaflets.

My hands tremble
with excitement
as I slip on my coat,
set my hat on my head,
step into the patrol car
that delivers me
to the university,
sirens blaring.

HUMMINGBIRD

Hans fidgets,
his knee bouncing
with incredible speed,
his gaze f l i t t i n g
around the room
like a caged bird.

I clear
my throat ever so
slightly to remind
him that
above all
we must
not
show
our fear.

EVIDENCE

Hans's elbow
bumps
my side,
he slips his
hand into his
pocket, pulls
out a folded
paper, begins
ripping it into
tiny
pieces.

Ach, Hans.

CAUGHT IN THE TRAP

With careful, slow movements,
Hans discreetly shreds
what he can, and I shift
in my seat, try to shield
his hand.

The first bits fall
to the ground noiseless
as snow, and Hans continues,
trying to free
his hands from treason.

You there!

And I fear
these deadly snowflakes
have just snapped
this trap
around us.

JAKOB SCHMID, CUSTODIAN

That student
has something in his hand.
He's trying to destroy it.

Herr Hefner
crosses the room
in two giant strides,
grabbing
the incriminating evidence
from the male student,
including
the shredded bits
dusting the floor
beside his shoes.

We collect the pieces,
hand them to the inspector
when he arrives,
cheeks pale,
eyes blazing.

My chest puffs
with pride
for the Vaterland
today.

GESTAPO HEADQUARTERS

Gestapo agents arrive,
handcuff us, lead us out
past the sea of students
that splits, with
half of them staring,
half averting their gazes
as we pass.

> Hans raises his voice,
> calls out to Gisela
>   standing
> with the rest of the
>   crowd,
> *Tell Alex I*
> *won't be around later.*

They yank us
toward the door
and the waiting police car
that whisks us away.

BEFORE

1943
Word from Fritz

Finally, a call, some news, a huge
sigh of relief.

Fritz lies in a field hospital
just outside of Stalino,
his frostbitten fingers
amputated,
but his frozen body
      alive,
at least for the moment.

Many others are
not. The capitulation
of Germany's Sixth Army tells
a truth clearer than any headline.
All those young, dead soldiers.

Germany cannot,
      should not
win this war.

We must fight
to ensure
its defeat.

THE PROFESSOR

A few of us gather
at the flat a week after the
spectacular defeat at Stalingrad
to discuss our next plans.

Professor Huber pulls
out a draft of a leaflet,
the first time he's shared
his own words with the group.

We listen,
eager and twitchy,
as he reads,

> Fellow Students! Our shocked people stand
> before the loss of men at Stalingrad.
> The ingenious strategy of
> the World War I corporal has led
> to the irresponsible and senseless deaths
> of three hundred thousand German men.
> Führer, we thank you!

We let out
a collective breath.
This is brilliant, forceful, bold.
Exactly what we need.

OUR SHAMEFUL ARMY

We're aglow with
excitement from the first lines of
the professor's leaflet,
but as he goes on, even I can see
that certain parts aren't
in line with what we aim
to accomplish.

Glances shoot
around the room
when the professor shares his hope
      that our glorious army
        might be saved.

Our glorious army fills
us with shame.

HANS AND ALEX

Hans and Alex wordlessly agree
to disagree
with the professor.

After an awkward pause, Hans speaks
for them both
      for us all
carefully asking if they can strike
a few lines, clearly hoping
he'll understand.

But Professor Huber frowns,
and it's hard to argue
with someone we asked to join
because we value
his opinion.

HEAVY WORDS

The professor shakes
his head, evidently not used
to such suggestions,
least of all from a student.

But I understand
why the boys won't
print it
exactly like this.

>   *Go ahead and destroy it then.*
>   The professor pushes
>   himself to standing,
>   heads
>   for the door.

We watch him leave,
his flimsy sheet of
paper bearing
a weight
as heavy
as a bomb.

DOING SOMETHING

After the professor leaves, I stuff
a small stack of
leaflets into my bag, pull
on my coat, slip
into the street, sleek
as an alley cat.

After sitting
on the sidelines
like a caged tiger
for a week,
I can't wait
to
        face my fears
to
        break out of my complacency
to
        do whatever I can.

I hunt
for deserted streets, leaving
leaflets on each car, inside
each telephone booth.

My heartbeat matches
the pounding of my heels over
the pavement as I turn
the corner.

Boom-boom,
boom-boom.

The rush is
undeniable.

TRANSFORMATION
Letter to Fritz, February 1943

Dear Fritz,

I was just back
home for a visit. *Home!*

The 150 kilometers between
Ulm and Munich
    transform
me until I arrive
    fully realized
    resolute
    ready.

But now that I'm here,
I can admit to you
(and only you) that
I'm still filled with fear.

I'm just as afraid for you.
It's been two weeks since
your letter from Stalino, and
even though I don't know
how you are, I'm filled
with love and gratitude knowing
you're at least alive.

MOUNTAINS OF PAPER

Breathless, I arrive
late after scouring
the city for all the
envelopes I could find.

There aren't nearly enough.

The boys have
been hard at work, the newest
leaflet in neat stacks piling
up next to the machine.

I read the same lines Hans used
from the professor's draft:

> Fellow Students!
> Our shocked people stand
> before the loss of men at Stalingrad.

My mind drifts,
zooming far to the north,
farther to the east,
to the field hospital where
Fritz still lies in grave danger.

All these young
lives sacrificed for the Reich—
this is why they wanted
Germany's youth in the first place.

MACHINES

Hans is a machine,
falling into the same rhythm
as the captivating beast in front of him,
　　　　inking the stencil
　　　　winding the crank
　　　　again and again.

Alex is a machine,
collecting the copies,
folding, stuffing, stacking.

Willi is a machine,
poring over lists of names,
typing envelopes, collecting
them in stacks by city.

If any of us are caught,
　　　　our parents
　　　　our siblings
　　　　our sweethearts
　　　　　　　will suffer.

But tonight my thoughts drift
to Christoph.

Christoph, with his
　　　　wife
　　　　small children
　　　　new baby.

Christoph, with so much more to lose,
with the Gestapo stepping
up efforts to find us,
with more soldiers on the streets,
more eyes watching everything.

Christoph isn't a machine at all,
but a thinking, sensitive soul, aware
his actions are a moral necessity, are
high treason, are
punishable by death.

I have no desire to die,
but I won't let my fear paralyze
me. Because like the others,
I too am a machine.

HANS'S IDEA

After we all push
ourselves to duplicate, fold, stuff
the leaflets into
all the envelopes we have,
huge stacks remain.

We stand and survey
the achievement like generals:
        Fifteen hundred?
        Two thousand?
        So many.

It's a good
problem to have.

                And Hans has a solution.
                What if we bring
                them to the university
                while classes are in
                        session?

PLANNING A REVOLUTION

I can barely control
my excitement about
Hans's idea,
but the others don't seem
to agree.

> *In broad daylight?*
> Alex says.
> *Too risky.*

Willi frowns, shakes
his head, his face blanching
pale as paper.

Even though the Gestapo must
be looking for us,
I'm so proud
of my brother,
so glad someone else thinks
as I do—
that we can always do more,
that we *should* always do more.

I for one am ready
to do more.

Leaflets
all around the university

in the bright light of day
for everyone to find
is simply brilliant.

Students will surely rise
and join us in this fight
once they know
the truth about the Vaterland.

THE END

FEBRUARY 22, 1943
If Words Could Kill

The trial will take place
        today
with the three of us
        Hans
        Christoph
        me
accused of
treason against
the Reich.

The defense attorney visits
my tiny, stale cell, and
after our first exchange, it's clear
he has no plans to provide
any useful defense.

Since he'll be no help in the
courtroom, perhaps he can be
of some help now, answering
the questions burning
through my mind.

If the verdict is the death
penalty, how will they do it?
Hanging, or guillotine?

What? He blanches,
his mouth dropping
like bomb bay doors.

*And what about my
brother? As a soldier, he deserves
a firing squad at the very least.*

Flustered, shaken, shocked,
the attorney sputters
to his feet, marches
for the door, refuses
to respond.

FREEDOM

After I read
my indictment, sign
my life away
on the bottom, I write
a single word—

    Freiheit—

on the back of the paper.

Across the room, my
cellmate has tears in
her eyes, but I turn
to the window, let
the sunshine warm
my face.

Such a lovely day.

But what does
my death matter
if it means
     more students will continue
     what we started
if it means
     our actions will start
     a revolution

if it means
    others might live?

The sun still shines.

I open my eyes, take
in the beauty that I know
lies beyond these walls, insert
my spirit into a sunbeam, send
a ray of hope into
this hopeless
world.

ELSE GEBEL, PRISONER

When they take Sophie
to stand trial, I wonder
if I'll ever see her again.

I'm already afraid I won't.

It was my job
to make sure
she didn't kill herself,
my job
to pay attention
to each and every word
my job
to gather
any information
that could incriminate
others.

But this young girl showed
such emotion
such conviction
such devotion
to her brother
that I couldn't imagine
betraying her.

ENEMY OF THE REICH

Handcuffed, hauled
down the corridor, treated
like a criminal,
now I have some idea
how it must have felt
to be
      Jewish
on Kristallnacht
or anytime since.

Shame burns
through me that we did
      nothing
to stop the beginnings of
the ugly wave of
      hate.

BEFORE

1938
Kristallnacht

I stand frozen
as torches light
up the night sky.

I think of Luise and my other
Jewish classmates, thankful
they already left Germany,
but other Jews still live
in Ulm, including
the Einsteins, no longer
in our building, but
not far away.

Right here, right now,
thumping boots fill
the streets with the first smash of
glass, deadly shards, inside and out.

Half of the faces on
the street light
up with glee,
the other half quake
in terror.

I feel only shame
that all I can do
is shudder, shiver, shut
my eyes.

I don't wait to find
out what's next to be
smashed, cut, burned.

Only one thought fills
me as I race home:

I
am
such
a
coward.

AFTERMATH

We don't do
anything,
not even with
      smashing glass
      the synagogue burning
people
      pushed into the street
      beaten, pummeled
      dragged to the banks of the Danube
huddling
indoors instead, identical grim
expressions on our faces.

We don't do
anything
to make it stop.

Vati goes out to check
on the Einsteins,
and I wonder
if there's something more
we can do.

But I don't
say
a word.

THE END

FEBRUARY 22, 1943
Roland Freisler, Judge

The interrogation transcripts
enrage me.

These corrupt youths!
These rotten traitors!
These terrible excuses for German citizens!

I will make sure they learn
that this Reich of ours
is no home
for rubbish like them.

They will pay for their impudence.
I enter the courtroom late,
right arm raised.

Heil Hitler.

FIRST, HANS

Guards lead all three of
us into the courtroom, past uniforms,
steely glances, heartlessness, and we take
our seats, pale and shaky.
Will any of us walk
away from this?

The judge of the People's Court
wastes no time calling
Hans forward, insulting
him for his
choices, his
actions, his
treason to the Reich.

Then he asks
why Christoph gave Hans
the draft they found
in his pocket.

> Hans stammers, clears his
> throat, speaks.
> *I asked him to write it.*
> *I told him what to say.*

But the judge bellows, his voice
reverberating off the walls

as he calls
all of us unworthy traitors,
and my brother trembles and I realize
nothing we say can save
any of us.

AUGUST KLEIN, DEFENSE ATTORNEY

Perhaps
if this boy
takes all the blame
the girl
can
escape
with her life.

MY BROTHER, THE PANZERFAUST

Hans
tries to stand
strong, but his fingers
still tremble.

Judge Freisler assails
my brother, gunning
him down with disgust at
the way we spread treason
against this mighty Reich
                          which will certainly fall
no matter what any naïve,
misinformed German thinks.

Hans takes
a deep breath, rigid
as a Panzerfaust, ready
to fire everything he's got
at the enemy tank in front of him.

He levels
his gaze to meet
the judge's cold, hard eyes.
                          Today you'll hang us,
                          but you
                          will be next.

The room goes
silent, and for a moment
it feels like
everyone
is
holding
a
collective
breath.

I could not be
prouder of my big brother.

ROLAND FREISLER, JUDGE

Of all the cowardly statements
I've heard
in all the proceedings
I've had the honor
to govern,
the useless words
falling
from the mouth
of this defendant
who calls himself a soldier
are perhaps
the most cowardly yet.

You're not
a German, not
a man. You're
only
a traitor.
Next witness.

I wait for his sister
to stand.

NEXT, ME

I've already made
my confession, don't understand why
we're here for this farce of a trial, except
to learn our punishment.

Still, the judge calls me
forward after putting
Hans under fire, demanding I explain
my actions, share my
shame with the court. I stand
tall and meet his gaze.

We did nothing
to be ashamed of,
and there's nothing
more to explain.
If I had to do it
all over again,
I'd do it
exactly the same.

I once loved
my country, but now the only
thing that shames
me is that I'm
German.

AUGUST KLEIN, DEFENSE ATTORNEY

I'll still
make a case
for a mild punishment
for the girl,
although
it'd be much easier
if she'd just
shut
her
mouth.

SILENCE

Judge Freisler asks
if I have any additional words.

Many others think
       the same,
they just don't say
          it.
But someone had to
make a start.

The judge laughs,
a bark from a vicious dog.

I turn, sweep
my gaze over the sea of
uniforms in the courtroom, breathe
in the heady silence, observe
the guilt shrouding
the audience, and I know
it's true.
          Even here,
          some do feel the same.

Say it,
I silently beg
my country,
this room full
of Germans.

But no one
says
a word.

ROLAND FREISLER, JUDGE

I've had enough
of this aggravating girl with
her accusatory gaze,
her superior tone,
her righteous attitude,
all of this puffing up
of her person as if
she knows
something I do not.

She
knows
nothing.

Next witness!

FINALLY, CHRISTOPH

Judge Freisler calls
Christoph, attacking him
for his own words
in the hastily scribbled draft
meant for only
Hans to see.

> How dare you
> refer to the Führer
> as a military con man
> while you call
> Roosevelt
> the strongest man in
> the world?

The judge bellows, showing
no mercy, and Christoph holds
a hand to his head, whispers,
I'm an unpolitical person.

Judge Freisler brandishes
the paper Hans so valiantly tried
to destroy, patched
back together, a completed
puzzle.

> But isn't this your
> handwriting?

Eyes blazing, he thrusts
the paper at Christoph,
who has nothing
he can say but
Yes.

FERDINAND SEIDL, DEFENSE ATTORNEY

I wouldn't choose
to defend
someone like
this young man
but was required
to do so
by order of
the People's Court.

The process goes
as expected.

The defendant's
own words
betray him
and there is
nothing
I can do
to save him,

even if
I wanted to.

THE CHILDREN

Christoph tries
to speak, tries
to respond,
and yet I can already see
that his pleas will do
no good.

In the end,
the judge's words beat him down—
   that narrow-minded thug,
clubbing
my friend with
pure National Socialist values.
Pure Scheiße.

In the end,
Christoph's last defense
is the one
that matters most:
     But . . . my children.

ROLAND FREISLER, JUDGE

Probst is a disgusting, sniveling excuse
of a German citizen.

His children are
irrelevant,
his arguments
immaterial.

Probst's children
are better off
without him.

A muscle twitches in my cheek.

I'm ready
to announce
my verdict.

BEFORE

1935
Rally at Nuremberg

We all watch Hans shoulder
his pack, chest puffed up
with enthusiasm as he heads
off to the rally as a flag bearer.

He's in for
      crowds
      ranks
      tents
      parades
      speeches.
He's in for
the time of his life.

Yet a week later, Hans returns
      subdued
      serious
      changed.

For the first time, a flicker of
doubt worms through me.
What if Vati
was right all along?

DISCIPLINED

I watch
my big brother, who's loved
     early-morning hikes
     camping with his troop
     stolen moments under the stars
     all in the fresh air
every bit as much as I have.

He's grown up in the
shadow of the swastika, has
been one of over a million
on the parade grounds at Nuremberg,
but when he has his squad design
their own special flag to show how
proud they are to be a part of
something so great, the leaders strip
him of his rank, disband
his squad.

Any

       individuality

is strictly

       forbidden.

NUREMBERG LAWS
September 1935

The Reichstag has unanimously
enacted the following laws.

1. The German Flag Law:
The flag of the German Reich is
red, white, black
with the swastika
of the National Socialist Party.

2. The Reich Citizenship Law:
Only those
of German blood
retain the right to
citizenship.
Jews are subjects of
the Reich and are not
eligible for citizenship.

3. The Law for the Protection of
German Blood and Honor:
Jews are prohibited
from marriage
and sexual intercourse
with citizens of German blood.

These laws go into
effect with this pronouncement.

The Führer and Reich Chancellor
Adolf Hitler

THE ARCHITECT OF IT ALL

One night at dinner Hans asks,
What's a concentration
camp?

We all crane
our necks toward
Vati at the head of the table.

He tells us of people hauled
off to terrible prisons without
standing trial, people
guilty simply for being:
a Communist
a Social Democrat
of a different political opinion.

But the Führer
doesn't know about
them,
does he? Inge asks.

My children,
Vati says,
who do you think
ordered
their construction?

We sit in
silence for the rest of
the meal, pushing
other thoughts out of
our heads.

THE END

VERDICT: FEBRUARY 22, 1943
Roland Freisler, Judge

In the name
of the German people
in the criminal case against
Hans Scholl
Sophie Scholl
Christoph Probst
the People's Court has determined that
the defendants, by means of treasonous
wartime leaflets,
have called for
sabotage
and the
collapse of the National Socialist
way of life,
propagated
defeatist thoughts,
shamelessly insulted
the Führer, thus favoring
the enemy of the Reich.
They are therefore sentenced
to death.

The accused forever forfeit
their honor as citizens
by their acts
of treason.

They bear the costs
of the proceedings.

Heil Hitler.

THREE TERRIBLE WORDS

Sentenced to death.

The words ring
in my ears, not surprising and
yet still, I shudder.

Sentenced to death.

Ice washes
over me in a bath of
sweat, cold as the Isar in winter.

Christoph.
My brother.
Me.

The three of us.

Sentenced
to
death.

A REALIZATION

Outrage roars
through me that not even
Christoph was spared and
the shock of it reverberates
through the courtroom, spiraling
over Munich, shooting
over Germany, hitting
the rest of the world
with full force.

They
are going to
murder
us.

I stand small in the wake
of this undisputable fact
as it slowly mixes
with a thin, silky ribbon flowing
through my thoughts, getting
bluer and brighter
than a clear sky
after a storm.

Our deaths
will mean
something.

The world will react,
and someday
someone
will punish
the people
who are doing
these terrible things.

The ribbon widens, flooding
my mind
with a river of hope.

AN UNWELCOME GUEST

Soldiers block
the entrance to the courtroom,
where a voice rises,
travels to us.

> *I'm their father.*

Vati. But here his words hold
no weight, useless as paper arrows trying
to besiege a fortress as he attempts
to push forward.

> *Get him out of here!*
> the judge bellows.

Soldiers pull him back,
but not before he gets a glimpse
of us, sitting
proud and tall as he taught us.

> *There is a higher justice!*
> Vati's voice echoes
> through the corridor
> as the doors
> slam shut.

ROLAND FREISLER, JUDGE

The impudence of those three youths—
especially that disrespectful, despicable girl—
makes me twitch even now,
as I sit alone in my chambers.

The girl's words echo through my head,
replaying that moment in the courtroom:
Someone had to
make a start.
Ridiculous.

Loathing rises in me,
and I push back from my desk
in an attempt to escape
the filthiness
of these pitiful prisoners.

By attempting to brainwash other young minds
at one of our finest universities
with their dangerous drivel,
these three enemies of the Reich
have ruined
their reputations and futures.
They will not haunt the purity
of my conscience.

BEFORE

1934
Round and Round

Hans and Vati are
at it again,
raised voices,
stony silences,
each bout more
uncomfortable than the last.

Vati's convinced
that a much greater evil lurks
in the plans of Herr Hitler
that reach beyond
the bread and freedom
of his campaign posters —
plans of
aggression
war
misery
death.

But Hans is right:
adults
simply don't understand
Herr Hitler's
belief
in a country
we couldn't love more.

Without a doubt,
the youth is the future
of this Reich,
a future that shines
bright as the sun.

MY BIG BROTHER

Every day Hans hangs up
the drawing on the wall
in the room he shares with Werner—
Adolf Hitler,
the new leader of the German Reich.

Every day
Vati takes it down,
rolls it up,
and places it
in a drawer.

Vati doesn't hide
his low opinion of the Führer,
calling him and his men wolves,
deceivers,
liars.

But Hans
wants to make his opinion heard.

Open the drawer,
pull it out,
hang it up.

LEAGUE OF GERMAN GIRLS

After months and months
of watching
my siblings go
off on merry adventures
with friends
flags
sports
I'm finally allowed
to join the Bund Deutscher Mädel
even though Vati
doesn't approve.

I excel
in the fresh air, leading
my own group
in my own way, making
sure we all share
our snacks equally,
though there are some girls
who grumble.

Others protest
when I turn in those who refuse
to attend required meetings.

But
rules
are
rules.

HANS AND VATI

Hans's daily arguments with Vati
have grown worse.

Hans defends our Führer proudly,
pointing at his promises
to end unemployment,
to build the Autobahn,
to put this great nation
to work.

Vati counters that these aims
will come at a price,
and that price
will be war.

I don't know
who will win.

CONFIRMATION

Mutti wants
to see me confirmed,
and I go to the church
wearing
my brown uniform
of the Bund Deutscher Mädel
instead of a scratchy black dress.

Filled with pride
in my uniform before
God, I raise
my eyes to the church's ceiling,
the heavens,
the greatness beyond.

MY JEWISH FRIENDS

I don't understand
why my friend Luise can't
join the BDM
when she has blond hair, blue eyes—
so decidedly Aryan—and I have
brown hair, brown eyes
(just like Herr Hitler).

I stand up
for the rights of my
Jewish classmates
to do as they wish,
though it seems they'd rather
I didn't.

THE END

FEBRUARY 22, 1943
Goodbye

They tell me I have
visitors—my parents—and I can't
get down the hall to
them quickly enough.

On my way to the door, Hans is led
out, his eyes glittering
like shiny stones.
Will I ever see him again?

I enter the visiting room, Vati pulls
me into his arms, tells
me what I want to hear.

You will go down in history.

This has to make waves,
I say, animated
by the weight of what we've done.

Mutti offers
me cookies, a reminder
of home, telling
me Hans didn't want any.

We haven't eaten.
Equal shares of courage and
matter-of-factness fill
my voice as I accept the sweets.

Because I am
courageous and
matter-of-fact
about what I hope
will happen now:

That the world will see
and the world will know
and the world
will
make
them
stop.

A PRAYER

I give
my parents
one last embrace, breathing
in the comfort they've given
me over all my years.

                Mutti releases me,
                tears in her eyes as she says,
                Remember, Sophie: Jesus,

and I know she wishes
me salvation.

But I also know
my suffering will be
quick while hers
will be
long, so I hold
back my own
tears and tell her,
You too.

HOME

Out in the corridor,
the tears I've been holding
back stream
down my cheeks as I picture
my family's dining table at
home in Ulm with
two chairs that will remain
        empty
forever.

Herr Mohr passes by, pales
at my tears, but so he doesn't think
I'm crying over
my own fate, I wipe
my cheeks, raise
my chin, tell him,
My parents.

LAST LETTER

Back in my cell,
a guard nods, thrusts
paper and pen at me, says,

> *Your last chance to say*
> *goodbye to anyone else*
> *is now.*

I begin

    Lieber Fritz

but can't find the words I seek
other than to tell
him how
      proud
I am of what we've done
how
      insistent
I am that I wouldn't
change
a thing.

A GIFT

A happy surprise
when the door creaks
open once more: the
guard again, this time ushering
in the best possible gift:
>Hans
>and
>Christoph.

The three of us rush
to embrace,
gasp, cling
to one another,
to our beliefs,
well
worth
this
sacrifice.

>*You've only got*
>*a few minutes.*
>The guard lights
>us a cigarette, closes
>the door.

We breathe
the heavy air, drawing
the last life
deep into our lungs.

TOGETHER

Hazy plumes of smoke from
the already extinguished cigarette drift
up to the corners of the cell, hanging
there like forgotten cobwebs.

Footsteps, and the
guard announces
my name
from the hallway.
                    Sophie Scholl.

It's then I realize
I need only survive
these
last
moments.

EXECUTION

The door opens
one last time, revealing
the executioner, dressed
    like an undertaker
    in a top hat and tails.

Hans and Christoph and I take
one another in one last time,
    proud
    strong
    brave,
and I know
dying will be so easy.

I leave them behind, follow wordlessly
across the courtyard
    to
    the
    blade.

Outside, I force
myself to forget, marveling
instead at the promise of
hope in the fresh February air and
a bird singing in a tree
beyond the wall, defying
winter's last chill and
the ugliness before me.

The execution room door yawns open then,
a dark, hungry mouth closing
in on me, surrounding
me with wood and metal and
the stench of death.

On the plank, I count
each breath in my mind—
        eins, zwei, drei—
until the last one floats
out of my lungs, dispersing
through the room,
and I'm flying.

EPILOGUE

1932
My Brother

We're out
of school for
the summer and
Hans bursts down the hall,
fishing rod and tackle in hand, calling
                    Freedom!

SOARING SKYWARD

Another lazy day lounging
beside the Iller with Werner,
  swimming
  drawing
  reading
but something makes
me look skyward
and a lonely falcon soars
  high
  higher
  highest
tipping its wings, reaching
for the heavens.

Majestic bird!

I can only hope
to one day become
such an inspiration.

AUTHOR'S NOTE

This story doesn't have a happy ending. Possibly the most tragic aspect of the White Rose group is that the executions of its members didn't "make waves" as Sophie had expected and so badly hoped. After the trial and execution of Sophie, Hans, and Christoph on February 22, 1943, the university community—like the rest of Germany—continued to cower under Hitler's regime. There was no revolt.

Instead, other friends were arrested for activities or association with the group. A second trial was held on April 19, 1943, resulting in prison sentences for Gisela Schertling, Traute Lafrenz, Hans Hirzel, and others, as well as death sentences for Alexander Schmorell, Willi Graf, and Kurt Huber. Alexander and Professor Huber were executed on July 13, 1943, and Willi on October 12, 1943.

The defeat of the German army at Stalingrad was the turning point of the war, but more than two long years of fighting and countless deaths still remained. Resistance within Germany might have brought about a swifter end to the war, but most people were simply too afraid for their own lives to act, especially after trials and executions like those of the White Rose members. The stakes were clear: resist, and you will be imprisoned or killed.

MY FIRST GLIMPSE

When I first heard about the White Rose in high school German class, I knew I wanted to learn more about its members. Sophie was the youngest and the only girl, and her courage made her a personal heroine and role model for me throughout the rest of my teen years. The more I studied the group, the more her tragically short life compelled me to tell her story. Seeing Sophie's letters and artwork in the Scholl archive at the Institute for Contemporary History on a trip to Munich and Ulm in 2005 brought her from my history books to life. She was truly a gifted artist. But I wanted to feel more than I could from books or archives. Trying to get inside Sophie's head that fateful day, I retraced her steps from the flat she shared with Hans on Franz-Josef-Strasse to the university, where I passed through the atrium, imagining Sophie and Hans placing stacks of leaflets outside the lecture hall doors, and headed up to the third-floor balustrade, where she stood and gave the leaflets a push. Finally, I visited Sophie's grave in the Perlacher Forest next to Stadelheim Prison, where she, Hans, and the others were laid to rest.

I began to work in earnest on the project just after this trip, focusing on the story as nonfiction, but set the project aside, unable to find the right format. Only ten years later, when I finally began the story in verse, did everything click into place.

FACT AND FICTION

In telling Sophie's story, I tried to stay as true to the known facts as possible, using details from my research in poetic interpretations of the material. Among the sources I studied were collections of letters to and from Hans, Sophie, and Fritz, the leaflets themselves, interrogation and trial paperwork, biographies of Sophie, books about the group, and published interviews with surviving family members and friends. These sources revealed not only facts about the group's resistance activities but also the personality, emotions, and convictions that helped me give Sophie her voice.

Most of the liberties I took with the story sprang from conflicting information across sources, a lack of details in any source, or a need to omit information Sophie wouldn't have known. These include details about Hans's sexuality, drug use by group members, Sophie's specific thoughts about the Holocaust, her initial involvement in the leaflet operation, and the final moments of the group before execution.

As always with historical research about deceased individuals, we don't know what the subject might have thought or said in private, particularly in a case like this, in which she had to make every effort to keep details of her work and her life a secret. Even close family and friends reported that they didn't know about Sophie's resistance activities. Combining the documented actions with the thoughts and feelings she did share, I tried to paint a full picture of her role in the resistance efforts, together with her character as a very real person.

LEGACY

Though Germans failed to stand up and revolt following the executions, one pair of students did continue the work of the White Rose. Hans Leipelt and his girlfriend, Marie-Luise Jahn, received a copy of the sixth leaflet, and after the executions on February 22, they added the line *und ihr Geist lebt trotzdem weiter,* "and their spirit lives on," to the top of the leaflet. They made copies and distributed them in Munich and Hamburg, resulting in their arrests in October 1943. At their trial a year later, Hans was sentenced to death and Marie-Luise to twelve years in prison. Hans was executed on January 29, 1945.

Smuggled leaflets also made it to the Allies, and more than five million copies were reprinted and dropped by aircraft over German cities. After the war, Inge's book *Die Weiße Rose* brought recognition to the group's actions, and countless other books and two successful films followed. Today there is a monument at the University of Munich honoring their resistance, and many streets and schools in Germany are named after White Rose members.

As Nobel Prize–winning author Thomas Mann said of Sophie and the rest of the group in a radio broadcast on June 27, 1943, "Good, splendid young people! You shall not have died in vain; you shall not be forgotten."

I truly hope I have given Sophie and the White Rose justice.

ACKNOWLEDGMENTS

The publication journey of a debut author is often a long and bumpy road, littered with shelved manuscripts, crumpled dreams, and broken bits of heart. To make it, we authors cling to what heart remains, soldier on, and firmly grip the hands of those who accompany us. So many people have helped me, both on my long writerly journey and on this particular book, and I hope beyond hope that I don't forget anyone here, because I couldn't have done it without all the support.

Immense thanks to Kwame Alexander and Margaret Raymo—as Kwame says, "You only need one yes," and I'm so very grateful that my yes came from the two of you, especially because Margaret's whip-smart vision was just what this book needed. Being part of the fantastic Versify lineup is a dream come true. Thank you also to the entire HMH and Versify team who helped turn this story into a real book, including Erika Turner, Margaret Wimberger, Mary Magrisso, and David Curtis and Sharismar Rodriguez for illustrating and designing the beautiful cover. An extra-sparkly special thanks to my magical agent, Roseanne Wells, for helping take my work to the next level, for supporting me every step of the way, and for believing in me even when I took a radical turn away from all the prose I'd written and began writing in verse, where I found my true calling.

I'll forever be indebted to the PEN/New England committee for choosing White Rose as a Discovery Award winner in 2017, as well as the Pitch Wars community for welcoming me into the fold, first as a mentee in 2014 and then as a mentor in 2016 and 2017. Thanks to Brenda Drake for all you do, Sarah

Guillory for being my favorite dementor, and the 2014 Pitch Wars class for being the absolute best. Thank you to my writing instructors over the years, including Padma Venkatraman, Alma Fullerton, Kathy Erskine, Holly Thompson, Carolyn Yoder, and Melanie Crowder; and danke to my high school German teacher, Frau Kellogg, and my Doktorvater, Professor Strelka, for all you taught me. Vielen Dank to the staff at the DenkStätte Weiße Rose and the Institut für Zeitgeschichte, and to all the authors whose books about the White Rose included in-depth research and interviews, many of those with surviving friends and family members. Special thanks to Barbara Leisner and Sönke Zankel for answering some specific questions.

To my critique partners and beta readers: thank you, thank you, thank you. To my original critique group, Joan Paquette, Julie Phillipps, and Natalie Lorenzi, and my longtime beta readers, Michelle Mason, Beth Smith, Shari Green, and JRo Brown —love you guys! To my *White Rose* readers, Kathy Quimby, Joy McCullough, Alexandra Alessandri, Marley Teter, Kerri Maher, Kristin Reynolds, Amanda Rawson Hill, Mara Rutherford, Sam Taylor, Carrie Callaghan, and Ann Braden—huge bucketloads of appreciation. To my sensitivity readers, Stephanie Cohen-Perez and a second reader who chose to remain anonymous—your insight was ridiculously helpful. Thank you. A huge shout-out to #5amwritersclub, where I do all my best work, to Rachel Simon for running the Boston crêpes group, and to the #novel19s for sharing this incredible year. And of course, to Monica Ropal, who reads everything I send, talks me off ledges, and pushes me to do better—don't ever leave me!

Finally, to the non-writerly people in my life. To my dad for encouraging my interest in German and history, and to my big brother, Matt, for being my own personal Hans. To my mom—love you and miss you and wish you were still here. To Rosanne Samson for distracting me with fun times and snacks, and to Casey Carlsen for inspiring me with beautiful strings of words. And, of course, to my own family—to my husband, Bernardo, for fixing broken Kips and for being my media naranja; to Megan for tagging along around Germany multiple times and for holding the microfilm; to Lyra for being witty and full of fun; and, last but not least, to Violeta for being the kindest, most bookish girl I've ever met. I'm so lucky to have you all in my corner! ¡Os quiero!

DRAMATIS PERSONAE

Roland Freisler (October 30, 1893–February 3, 1945) was a judge with the Third Reich and president of the People's Court, infamous for humiliating defendants and sentencing them to death. He was killed during an air raid on Berlin.

Clemens August Graf von Galen (March 16, 1878–March 22, 1946) was a Catholic bishop who protested the Third Reich's euthanasia program in his sermons.

Else Gebel was a political prisoner who shared Sophie's cell.

Willi Graf (January 2, 1918–October 12, 1943) was a German medical student and a member of the White Rose resistance group. He was arrested on February 18, stood trial on April 19, and was executed by guillotine at Stadelheim Prison in Munich on October 12, 1943.

Fritz Hartnagel (February 4, 1917–April 29, 2001) was a German army officer and close friend of the Scholl family. He was Sophie's on-and-off boyfriend, and they maintained an intense letter exchange up until her execution. After the war and through their joint grief, Fritz and Sophie's sister Liesl became much closer and married.

Hans Hirzel (October 30, 1924–June 3, 2006) was a high school student and the younger brother of one of Sophie's friends from Ulm. He purchased a duplicating machine with money from Sophie and distributed leaflets she brought him in Ulm. He was arrested by the Gestapo, stood trial on April 19, 1943, and was sentenced to five years in prison.

Kurt Huber (October 24, 1893–July 13, 1943) was a German philosophy professor and a member of the White Rose resistance group. He was arrested on February 27, stood trial on April 19, and was executed by guillotine at Stadelheim Prison in Munich on July 13, 1943.

August Klein was appointed by the People's Court as the defense attorney for Hans and Sophie Scholl.

Traute Lafrenz was a German medical student, one of Hans's girlfriends, and a member of the White Rose resistance group. She was arrested on March 15, 1943, stood trial on April 19, and was sentenced to a year in prison.

Anton Mahler was an interrogator with the Gestapo during the Third Reich who interrogated Hans Scholl, among others.

Robert Mohr (April 5, 1897–February 5, 1977) was an investigator and interrogator with the Gestapo during the Third Reich who led the manhunt for the White Rose and then interrogated Sophie Scholl and Christoph Probst, among others. After the war he was briefly interned by the Allies but was not brought to trial for his role in the Gestapo.

Christoph Probst (November 6, 1919–February 22, 1943) was a German medical student and a member of the White Rose resistance group. In spite of his young age, he was married and a father of three. He was executed by guillotine at Stadelheim Prison in Munich on February 22, 1943.

Herta Probst (July 21, 1914–September 21, 2016) was the wife of Christoph Probst and the mother of his three children.

Gisela Schertling (February 9, 1922–November 8, 1994) was a loyal National Socialist but was also a close friend of Sophie and was one of Hans's girlfriends. Though not directly involved in the White Rose's resistance activities, she was aware of what they were doing and looked the other way. She stood trial on April 19 and was sentenced to a year in prison.

Jakob Schmid was the custodian at the University of Munich who witnessed Hans and Sophie upstairs when the leaflets fell into the atrium. He promptly arrested them and delivered them to his superior, who called the Gestapo.

Alexander Schmorell (September 16, 1917–July 13, 1943) was a German medical student and a member of the White Rose resistance group. He fled when he heard of the others' arrests but was captured on February 24, stood trial on April 19, and was executed by guillotine at Stadelheim Prison in Munich on July 13, 1943.

Elisabeth (Liesl) Scholl (February 27, 1920) is the middle Scholl sibling. She married Sophie's boyfriend, Fritz, after the war ended.

Hans Scholl (September 22, 1918–February 22, 1943) was a German medical student and a member of the White Rose resistance group. He was executed by guillotine at Stadelheim Prison in Munich on February 22, 1943.

Inge Scholl (August 11, 1917–September 4, 1998) was the older sister of Hans and Sophie Scholl.

Robert Scholl (April 13, 1891–October 25, 1973) was the father of Hans and Sophie Scholl and their three siblings, Inge, Elisabeth, and Werner. A former mayor, he was outspoken against Hitler and the National Socialist Party from the onset and was imprisoned for speaking out in 1942.

Sophie Scholl (May 9, 1921–February 22, 1943) was a German biology and philosophy student, the younger sister of Hans Scholl, and a member of the White Rose resistance group. She was executed by guillotine at Stadelheim Prison in Munich on February 22, 1943.

Werner Scholl (November 13, 1922–June 1944) was the younger brother of Hans and Sophie Scholl. He went missing on the Russian front in 1944 and is presumed dead.

Ferdinand Seidl was appointed by the People's Court as the defense attorney for Christoph Probst.

GLOSSARY

Arbeitsdienst: Labor service (see Reichsarbeitsdienst below).

bitte: Please.

Blitzkrieg: Literally "lightning war," this signifies the importance of shock, strength, and speed in an all-out attack by military forces.

Bund Deutscher Mädel: League of German Girls, the girls' branch of the Hitler Youth.

danke: Thanks.

danke schön: Thanks a lot.

Deutschland: Germany.

Deutschland über alles: "Germany above all," a line from the German national anthem.

eins, zwei, drei: One, two, three.

Freiheit: Freedom.

frische Luft: Fresh air.

Führer: Leader.

Hauptbahnhof: Main train station.

Hitlerjugend: Hitler Youth.

Iller: A river in Ulm.

Isar: A river in Munich.

Jude: A Jewish person.

Kinder, Küche, Kirche: "Children, kitchen, church," this phrase was used to express the pillars that were seen as the ideals for German women.

Kristallnacht: "Night of Broken Glass" (November 9–10, 1938), during which Jewish businesses and people were attacked and synagogues were burned.

Münster: Cathedral.

nein: No.

Nieder mit Hitler: "Down with Hitler."

OKW Bericht: Armed forces report.

Panzerfaust: Bazooka.

Pervitin Wachhaltemittel: An alertness drug, methamphetamine.

Reich: Empire, nation.

Reichsarbeitsdienst: National Labor Service.

Reichsmark: National mark, German unit of currency from 1924 to 1948.

Scheiße: Shit.

Sitzkrieg: Literally "sitting war," this signifies the period between the German invasion of Poland on September 3, 1939, and the attack on the western front on May 10, 1940, during which no new attacks began.

Vaterland: Fatherland, homeland.

Volk: People, folk.

Wehrmacht: German armed forces from 1935 to 1946.

SELECTED SOURCES

SOURCES IN ENGLISH

Most sources about the White Rose are available in German only. The following resources are excellent starting points for non-German speakers who'd like to know more.

Dumbach, Annette, and Jud Newborn. *Sophie Scholl and the White Rose.* Oxford: Oneworld Productions, 2006.

Gedenkstätte Deutscher Widerstand [German Resistance Memorial Center]. https://www.gdw-berlin.de/en/recess/topics/15-the-white-rose/.

Jens, Inge, ed. *At the Heart of the White Rose: Letters and Diaries of Hans and Sophie Scholl.* New York: Harper & Row, 1987.

Johnson, Eric, and Karl-Heinz Reuband. *What We Knew: Terror, Mass Murder, and Everyday Life in Nazi Germany.* Cambridge, MA: Basic Books, 2005.

Kater, Michael. *Hitler Youth.* Cambridge, MA: Harvard University Press, 2004.

McDonough, Frank. *Sophie Scholl: The Real Story of the Woman Who Defied Hitler.* Gloucestershire, UK: History Press, 2010.

Scholl, Inge. *The White Rose.* Translated by Arthur Schultz. Middletown, CT: Wesleyan University Press, 1970.

United States Holocaust Museum. https://collections.ushmm.org/search/.

The following films are available with English subtitles:

Rothemund, Marc, and Fred Breinersdorfer. *Sophie Scholl: Die Letzten Tage* [Sophie Scholl: The last days]. X Verleih AG, 2005.

Verhoeven, Michael, and Mario Krebs. *Die Weiße Rose* [The White Rose]. CCC Film, 1982.

PRIMARY SOURCES IN GERMAN

The following German sources were invaluable to me. These collections of primary sources include letters, diaries, interviews, and other documents.

ALEX: Historische Österreichische Rechts-und Gesetztext Online [ALEX: Historical Austrian Legislation and Law Text Online]. http://alex.onb. ac.at/cgi-content/alex-iv.pl?aid=dra.

Bassler, Sibylle. *Die Weiße Rose: Zeitzeugen erinnern sich* [The White Rose: Eyewitnesses remember]. Bremen: Rowohlt Verlag, 2006.

Chaussy, Ulrich, and Gerd R. Ueberschär. *Es lebe die Freiheit! Die Geschichte der Weißen Rose und ihrer Mitglieder in Dokumenten und Berichten,* 2 Auflage [Long live freedom! The history of the White Rose and its members in documents and reports, second edition]. Frankfurt/Main: Fischer Verlag, 2013.

Hartnagel, Thomas, ed. *Sophie Scholl. Fritz Hartnagel: Damit wir uns nicht verlieren* [Sophie Scholl. Fritz Hartnagel: So that we don't lose one another]. Frankfurt am Main:, Fischer Verlag, 2005.

Jens, Inge, ed. *Hans Scholl. Sophie Scholl. Briefe und Aufzeichnungen* [Hans Scholl. Sophie Scholl. Letters and diaries]. Frankfurt am Main: Fischer Verlag, 1984.

———. *Willi Graf: Briefe und Aufzeichnungen* [Willi Graf: Letters and diaries]. Frankfurt am Main: Fischer Verlag, 2004.

Moll, Christiane, ed. *Alexander Schmorell. Christoph Probst: Gesammelte Briefe* [Alexander Schmorell. Christoph Probst: Collected letters]. Berlin: Lukas Verlag, 2011.

SECONDARY SOURCES IN GERMAN

The following German secondary sources include detailed biographies and books about the group as a whole:

Beuys, Barbara. *Sophie Scholl: Biografie* [Sophie Scholl. Biography]. Munich: Carl Hanser Verlag, 2010.

Gebhardt, Miriam. *Die Weiße Rose: Wie aus ganz normalen Deutschen Wiederstandskämpfer wurden* [The White Rose: How ordinary Germans became resistance fighters]. Munich: Deutscher Verlagsanstalt, 2017.

Gottschalk, Maren. *Schluss. Jetzt werde ich etwas tun,* 2. Auflage [That's it. Now I'm going to do something, second edition]. Weinheim: Beltz & Gelberg, 2016.

Leisner, Barbara. *Ich würde es genauso wieder machen: Sophie Scholl* [I'd do it exactly the same again: Sophie Scholl]. Berlin: List Taschenbuch, 2005.

LeMO (Lebendiges Museum Online), Jahreschronik [Living History Museum, Historical Milestones]. http://www.dhm.de/lemo/jahreschronik/.

Scholl, Inge. *Die Weiße Rose* [The White Rose]. Frankfurt am Main: Fischer Taschenbuch Verlag, 1955.

Vinke, Hermann. *Das kurze Leben der Sophie Scholl* [The short life of Sophie Scholl]. Ulm: Ravensburger Buchverlag, 1987.

———. *Fritz Hartnagel: Der Freund von Sophie Scholl* [Fritz Hartnagel: Sophie Scholl's boyfriend]. Zürich-Hamburg: Arche Verlag, 2005.

Zankel, Sönke. *Die Weisse Rose war nur Anfang* [The White Rose was only the beginning]. Köln: Böhlau Verlag, 2006.

MORE BOOKS
FROM VERSIFY

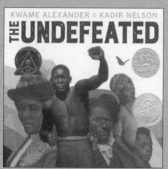

CHANGE THE WORLD, ONE WORD AT A TIME.